Best Wis

John Holmes

Three Dark Jewels

JOHN M HOLMES

DEDICATION

This book is dedicated to Donald Cannon

CONTENTS

"*Her dark jewels do hang like burnished coal*
Across the fabric of approaching night."

Lady Claire Spellman, Duchess of Kent, 1724

OLD POISON

Chapter 1 Thursday - 1:35 P.M. Nov. 1968

Lylah pulled into the school parking lot and noticed a line of dark clouds beginning to bank up along the horizon north of Rosemont. According to forecasts, nasty weather was heading this way tonight. A chorus of fifth graders, singing a song about rabbits, assaulted her ears as she entered the school. She instantly recalled singing it herself nearly- god, could it really be forty years ago?

"The bunnies ran hippity hop, hippity hop, all across the glen/ We'll never see them hippity hop ever, ever again. . ." What was it supposed to mean, anyway? She struggled to remember the sense of the story in the song but couldn't. Only its irritating melody lingered, disturbing, like an unwelcome visitor from the past.

She knew the way to the guidance office by now, ignored the secretary in the glass enclosed office she passed, and had her hand on the right door knob before anyone spotted her. Her eleven year old daughter, Irene, sat, forlorn and borderline bereft, across the desk from Brenda Shade, counselor.

"What's happened, Mrs. Shade?"

"Mrs. Todd, please have a seat. Irene, maybe it would be better if you told your mother what happened in the cafeteria."

She tried easing herself down into a modernistic white plastic chair, pulling it a little closer to her daughter as she did so.

"Dear me, did something happen at lunch? Can't you even eat without causing a problem, honey?"

The girl began speaking, but her voice was a low, trembling whisper her mother could barely hear.

"Darling, will you speak up? We're not in church, you know."

The girl shifted her weight a bit in her chair, brushed strands of her blonde hair back from her ear and looked directly at her mother.

"We never go to church, mom."

"You know that's not really true - " She darted a guilty glance at the counselor.

"Now, Irene, just tell your mother -"

A seemingly endless stream of words, sounding almost carefully rehearsed, came pouring out into the little cramped room.

"We were standing in the food line with our trays when Sherry, who was right in front of me, dropped one of her books. I stopped to pick it up for her and our hands touched. So that, of course, was when my lights started flashing and blinking, and so I knew a vision was coming. A few seconds later – "

A look of pure dread began to take shape across Mrs. Todd's face.

"- even before the lady put our sodas on our trays, I started receiving it, and it was so strong, mother, so very strong I just had to blurt it out to Sherry. You're going to die, Sherry. I just saw it - you're going to be killed in a car crash at the age of twenty-two!" Then Sherry started screaming, and some of the other kids were saying I was being a freak again. One of the boys grabbed my hair and

10

Peggy Fedor got a ketchup container and squirted it all over my face - people should be punished, paid back for doing bad things, shouldn't they?"

At this point Mrs. Shade came around to the two of them, at a loss to know which one to console first. She informed the girl's mother she had helped Irene clean herself up. It was Coach Markle who settled things down in the lunchroom. Sherry's father was called and came and took his hysterical daughter home for the rest of the day.

"He's a good friend of your husband, isn't he?" asked Mrs. Shade.

"Yes," she replied, wiping tears away, looking at the pathetic hulk next to her. "The Trekkers have been our friends for years. This is the first time anything like this has happened outside our home . We've had her to see a specialist on seizure disorders, but - "

"When I told Sherry's dad you'd be coming in soon for a conference regarding the incident, he asked me to - well, ask YOU to phone him later. Said he wants you to know he's not angry but would like to talk to you about something his daughter told him about Irene. Would you need his number? I understand he's a highly regarded professor at Rosemont College, and we always encourage our parents to keep all channels open. He does seem eager to talk to you, Mrs. Todd."

"Thank you, Mrs. Shade. We have his number."

"Please, it's Brenda. I'm sure we can be on a first name basis, - Lylah, isn't it?"

"Of course - Brenda. Should I take her home for the rest of the day?"

"Yes, but actually Mr. Warren requests you keep her home until Monday, and we were wondering if you and your husband could drop in on Saturday for a session with us about the entire matter - say at 10:30?"

To Mrs. Todd, this sounded like trouble, but she felt in no position to question the school's procedure. Sensing the approach of one of her headaches, she agreed to see Mr. Warren at the suggested time and reached across to her daughter.

"Come along, Irene. You can come with me to my doctor's appointment."

The girl flinched, pulled back.

"Don't go, Mom -cancel it."

"Oh, my, what an idea- cancel it!"

Pulling her out into the hall, she felt caught up in a whirl of anxiety. Mother and daughter exited Good Shepherd School for a walk to the parking lot. Lylah heard the girl moaning that there was something wrong with the air, she could smell a rotten odor in the breeze.

"You might have the makings of a meteorologist, honey - like the weather girl on TV."

"You're making fun of me again. Daddy told you to stop doing that."

"I don't mean to make fun, sweetie, I'm only trying to change the subject."

Once in the car, the girl sat in a crouch, casting furtive looks every few seconds outside and then to the left at her mother.

"Sit up straight," said Lylah , starting the car and aiming it out of the visitors' lot.

"What time is your appointment?"

"Two-thirty."

"Don't go."

"Why on earth not?"

"Do us all a favor. Brick wall with green leaves crawling up to the top."

Lylah pressed her foot down hard on the brake and pulled over. They'd only traveled a block from the school.

"Shut up, shut up, shut up! There - I'm not making fun of you. I'm just begging for a little peace. I need a cigarette - I'll even let you have one."

The girl , astonished, sat bolt upright.

"Poison," she said, just the one word.

Her mother dropped an unlit Marlboro to the floor of the car.

"What are you talking about?"

"Miss Lane says they're not good for you, said cigarettes are poison. Worse than poison Ivy, even."

"Oh yeah!"

"Yeah, and that most plants and flowers are nice - harmless, but just like people - some of them are dangerous. The Venus fly trap - "

Her mother interrupted.

"That, I would say, is an extreme example, darling."

"But Mom - " Ablaze now with a new interest, she could not be stopped.
"There are some flowers that can be boiled and will actually kill you if you drink it. It happened, it happened to some Roman king or somebody."

Lylah was suddenly hot, so even though it was November, she cranked her window open and puffed away on her cigarette.

"Really, Irene, I don't know why Miss Lane is filling your head with all this - "

"I think it's called education, mom. It takes my mind off all this other stuff that gets into my head and worries me. And yesterday she showed us pictures of ancient Egypt, mummies and their gods and everything- and I told the class about the stone our great aunt Mildred gave your mother, the one you said she got from an Egyptian tomb, and - "

Lylah was crying now, a long stream of tears sliding down her cheek. She instinctively stroked her daughter's hair in a gesture of comfort.

"Oh, sweetheart, when I finish up with Doctor Barrow today, I think it's time your father and I find a doctor to help you out as well. Once you have a doctor of your own, he'll clear up that mess you've got in your head. But you shouldn't mention our family business to your class.

Whatever got into you - bringing up Cousin - she was a distant cousin - Mildred's silly stone?"

"You and Daddy said it's supposed to be hundreds and hundreds of years old, and it's from Egypt, and Miss Lane was showing us pictures of the Pharaohs and the mummies, so I just raised my hand, and Miss Lane said for me to ask if I can bring it in for show and tell. Can I?"

Irene reached out and turned on the radio while her mother inhaled the cigarette. Simon and Garfunkel's "Mrs. Robinson" was strumming away.

"Oh!" Irene's mother almost squealed with pleasure. "Your father and I just saw that movie last week."

"Daddy went to see a musical?"

"No, it's not a musical. But they use a couple of their songs as background music."

"Will you buy me the record?"

"I will - if you wait quietly for me in Dr. Barrow's office until I come out. Do we have a deal?"

"Of course we have a deal. Just drive carefully, and if you see a brick wall with green leafy plants growing up to the top, pull over, okay?"

Reluctantly, Lylah's face lit up with smile.

"Oh, you're my little funny bunny," she said as she put the car in drive and pulled out onto the road.

"Speaking of bunnies," she said, and asked her daughter how that rabbit song the little kids were singing ended.

"I remember singing it myself when I was a little girl. How does the song finish up? What happens to those crazy bunnies, any way?"

"All the hunters track them down and shoot them, mom."

The car slowed down, and Lylah turned the radio off abruptly.The familiar anxiety settled over both of them like a cloud as they coasted along Main Street. Seated next to Lylah, the child sang the end of that awful nursery tune.

"The hunters' wives cooked a rabbit stew, a rabbit stew, a rabbit stew/ Will there be enough for me and you, me and you, me and you?"

Chapter 2 - Ten Minutes Later

Barrow's secretary, a short-haired blonde in a miniskirt Lylah thought inappropriate for her position, complimented her on her punctuality, smiled sweetly at both, then opened the door to the doctor's office. Lylah first showed Irene to a chair near a rack of children's magazines and books, before following Miss Sipple into the adjoining room.

Even before the shock of seeing her husband in the doctor's office, she saw the framed watercolor painting of a red brick wall, at least half covered with twisty strands of ivy, hanging on the wall above his head. When Jerry stood and extended his hand toward her, she nearly collapsed.

"What are you d-doing here? What about your afternoon classes?"

"I phoned him at the high school two hours ago and asked him to be here, Lylah," said the doctor.

Jerry held her close and whispered that there was bad news, but that they would get through it together. She saw something she'd never seen in his handsome face before. His dimpled, boyish smile was nowhere visible - only this odd mask of worried concern. What was this all about? Now Barrow too, was fussing around her and helping her to sit.

"What's happened? What's going on?"

"The results of the x-rays revealed a tumor on the brain," the doctor began. "That was the cause of your headaches and dizzy spells. It's deeply embedded, and its location makes it inoperable. I'm sorry, Lylah."

"And that means what?" she asked, feeling her husband's fingers tightening around her own.

"The prognosis is, unfortunately, not good."

"Prognosis . . ."

Her voice was trailing off, and she could almost feel her heart making the connection before her mind. She saw the doctor's lips moving, knew he was speaking, but couldn't even hear his voice for the rushing sound of waves washing up on a beach somewhere nearby- or was it a river, a wide one with palm trees all along the banks? Where was she, anyway?

Now she saw it all - this was her deserved punishment, the thing she had been anticipating for years. Filled with a need to hurl herself out of the nearest window, she looked around frantically, but saw that there were no windows - no escape at all. Even that wretched painting on the wall presented nothing but an obstacle.

Some words, though, break through anything, and the doctor's next ones certainly did.

"I think we can guarantee you a few months, Lylah, but perhaps not much more. Of course you can get a second opinion."

She saw Jerry's eyes full of tears.

"Poor Jerry," she said, touching his cheek with her unsteady hand.

Then, of all things, Miss Sipple swung the door open from behind them. There was a wild look in her eyes.

"Doctor, I just stepped out into the hall for a few seconds, and when I came back - "

Her arm extended back toward the waiting room as an invitation for them to see what she had seen. All three, confused, hurried out of the office.

A foot below the ceiling, cradled in the curved metal rods of a faux-colonial chandelier, little Irene lay still ,and seemingly unconscious, in mid-air as it were, at least seven feet above the floor. There was nothing below her that could explain how she had elevated herself to that height. As both men reached up to untangle her from her nest, Miss Sipple made a move to grab one of the nearby chairs. It was then that Lylah did the only sensible thing, and allowed herself the release of fainting, to the floor.

Dr. Barrow, Jerry and the secretary managed to carry both mother and daughter back into the office and examination room. They'd dislodged the overhead lamp a bit from the ceiling, causing it to swing back and forth for a while.

Chapter 3 - Prescott Medical College
Sacklear Dormitory - one hour later

Gary Todd napped with the same formula he applied to nearly everything else: planning, purpose and determination. His father had often told him he'd acquired these traits from his deceased mother, Vera, who died when the boy was seven. His classes this year were so demanding, he realized if he didn't take an hour nap before the dinner bell sounded at 5:30 that he would never be alert enough to put in the necessary study time at the campus library in the evening. This was by now a daily ritual for him, and he had become as addicted to the late afternoon "shut-downs," as he called them, as alcoholics to their after-work martinis.

So just after 4:15 the sneakers came off and he stretched himself out on the narrow bed and closed his eyes. His room mate, Chip, had quickly learned to enter quietly if he entered between 4 and 5:30, and learned too not to wake him. Chip was a mere freshman, whose primary concern was to pass all his courses and become a sophomore. He had sensed right from the start that Gary, a year ahead of him, was bright, and someone who might be a good friend to have for the next couple of years. If that meant deferring to him regarding his stupid nap policy, he figured it might be worth it. Besides, Gary was in great shape, had cannonball biceps, and could no doubt pulverize Chip in any altercation that might arise.

Chip came into their room around 4:15, saw Gary already in a serious snooze , placed his biology text and notebook on his desk and quietly headed toward the bathroom. Two minutes later when he came out, he heard the ringing telephone from the end of their hall.

On his bed, Gary opened his eyes and asked Chip to please be a good buddy and run down to pick it up.

"Sure thing, sleeping beauty. Your wish is my command."

"You're mixing your fairy tales, Chipster."

"And I guess you'd be the expert on fairies, now, wouldn't you?"

Chip enjoyed the teasing banter they had developed over the past couple of months and felt confident a genuine friendship was beginning. As an only child, he was finally realizing what he had been missing in not having a sibling. So he was grinning with satisfaction by the time he reached the third floor phone booth at the end of the hall.

Much to his surprise, the caller was Gary's dad, wanting to speak to his son- if he was in.

"Sure, Mr. Todd, he's in . This is Chip - his room mate. I'll get him."

"Hey, Gary, rise and shine!" he called out as he re-entered. "It's your dad."

Instantly alert, Gary was off in a flash, shuffling out in his stocking feet, wondering what could have happened to make his father feel the need to call. Occasionally his step mother would call just to see how he was doing. Especially last year, his first year at Med school. But his dad had never called - at least until now. Something was definitely up.

"Hi, Dad, what's goin' on?"

"Your mother -"

"Step," he hated himself right away for interrupting, so he quickly added, "Sorry, Dad."

"Lylah and your sister both had a rough day. Your STEP mother got some bad news from the doctor regarding her headaches, and Irene went into one of her trances, so Dr. Barrow sent her to the hospital for observation. I'm there now, and I think Lylah is planning to spend the night here - the nurse just told me it'll be okay."

"Should I come home?"

"I thought that since tomorrow's Friday, maybe you could cut classes and come home for a long weekend. I could drive you back on Sunday."

"What kind of bad news did my stepmother get, exactly?"

"We'll talk about it when I see you."

"I've got no tests tomorrow. I'll get a ride from someone and see you late tonight. Should I go to the hospital?"

"No, go to the house, and I'll be home by eleven. They're forecasting some storms are on the way, so be careful - and thanks, Gary."

When he got back to his room, he asked Chip what kind of shape his car was in.

"Zoom, zoom, zoom - ready to go, man. Need to borrow it?"

"No, wouldn't want to deprive you of your wheels for the weekend- thought maybe you could just drive me home - like it's only fifty miles. Just drop me off, and - if we leave right after dinner, you'd still be back here by midnight? Think you can help me out?"

Chip managed to hide his thrill at being asked behind a serious expression.

"Sure, man," then added, "Something wrong on the home front?"

"My dopey sister's acting up again, and my stepmother's got a problem with her headaches. My dad sounds bent out of shape.

Let's go down and see if we can get some early chow from Big Chef Dave, and be on our way - okay?"

Chapter 4 - Hospital Room 10 minutes Later

Jerry wondered if he'd be able to deal with this mess, this one-two punch they'd received today. The awful news regarding the tumor, and then this incredible recurrence of Irene's blackouts or trances - whatever the hell they were. He couldn't begin to imagine how she had gotten herself up into that crazy lamp.

But he was sitting next to Lylah now, holding her hand, so he knew he was getting things right so far. He was by her side, together with her, both of them at Irene's bedside in case she should snap out of it - whatever the "it" was.

Barrow had ordered x-rays of the child's brain and said he'd read them in the morning, then see Jerry and Lylah back here at the hospital to discuss what further steps might be taken. And before leaving them in the room nearly two hours ago, he had told them to notify one of the nurses if they observed even the slightest change in Irene's level of awareness. Now his wife startled him somewhat by withdrawing her hand from his.

"I think I'll take a quick drive home and get some things so I can spend the night - you'll stay here with her til I get back?"

"Of course."

"And Gary's coming home tonight, is that right?"

"That's what he said."

"I should be back - "

She cast a worried glance back at Irene.

"Lylah, I won't fall asleep, don't worry. Just drive carefully in this weather."

Now in the doorway, she turned back, hesitant, distracted.

"Oh," she said, "I forgot. Steve Trekker wants to talk to me about the incident at the school today. Mrs. Shade thinks he might be able to help or something. What do you think?"

"Yeah, Steve's a good guy. Call him before you come back, honey."

So he sat alone, watched streams of rain pelting the dark window glass and heard the familiar sounds of passing traffic on Crawford Boulevard.

His daughter, lying on her back under a white sheet pulled tight up to her shoulders, had been completely motionless for hours. Moving into the vacant chair Lylah had been sitting in, he reached out and clasped Irene's little twig-like fingers. What was wrong with his pathetic little girl?

Then he saw her lips part - had he really seen it? Yes, they were closing now - and look, her eye lashes had just fluttered, hadn't they? He was about to call for a nurse when she spoke just one word - a word he hadn't heard in years, a name of someone his little girl had never met, probably never even heard mentioned. And she spoke it clearly, distinctly - though with her eyes still shut - the first name of his first wife: "Vera."

Spellbound, Jerry leaned in closer.

"What is it, sweetheart? Daddy's listening."

There was a strange, deep resonance to the girl's voice now.

"She's too stupid to notice any change in the coffee's flavor."

"What, honey?"

"I SAID - " and now the voice sounded familiar, exactly like one he'd been listening to for years. " I said she's too stupid to notice something I added to her coffee . . ."

The girl's eyes were still closed. But the voice, that voice, continued.

"I read about it. It's supposed to have a bitter taste, but I can stir in some sugar along with it. The hospital will never notice it's gone, and Vera won't notice I added it to her coffee, either. Nobody ever notices anything, at least not the right things. She's pretty, though, I'll say one thing for him - he knows how to pick them. Yes, sir."

Jerry felt gripped by a panic and an unease more intense than his feelings earlier when he got the news about Lylah and then saw his daughter lying above their heads in the ceiling lamp. A rumble of thunder caused a chill to creep up his spine. Or could it have been caused by Irene - energy transferred from whatever was going on inside her strange brain to his.

Well, he thought, she is my daughter, "flesh of my flesh," as they say.

Now that voice again, the voice that didn't match the face it was coming from:

"How old is your boy, Vera? . . . Oh, that's a good age I'll bet. I hope to have some of my own one day, too. . . Oh, he's a handsome little fellow, looks very much like his dad - where was it taken?"

Her fingers twisted under his own, so he released his hold on them slightly. Then he asked her what she took from the bottle.

"White pills - digitalis. I crushed them down into a powder."

He asked her where she got it.

23

"From the dispensary."

He knew that word, too, was way beyond her vocabulary level as a fifth grader, but the voice, of course, was Lylah's, who had been a nurse years ago when they first met. As a matter of fact - he looked around as though something had clicked into place - this was the very same hospital, Rosemont Mercy, where she worked years ago. And it was also the hospital where his first wife worked in the billing department, until that awful day she was stricken by a heart attack.

Yes, Vera had died in this very hospital. Jerry felt his throat begin to constrict as these matters swam round his brain. Had Lylah known Vera , perhaps met her here in their common workplace? If so, Lylah had never told him about it - or had she?

His daughter was resting quietly again, so he got up to walk down the hall to the nurses' station. On his way, he was shifting his mind back to those days a dozen or so years ago when he first began seeing Lylah regularly.

********** **********
.

Hadn't he first met Lylah in the big supermarket just down the street here on Crawford Boulevard? It was plain Crawford Street then, a few years before it was widened into a four-lane highway to become a boulevard. A new wide screen movie theater had recently been built next to the market, and two or three days after he first noticed her long fingers grab a plastic wrapped head of lettuce at the market, they waited in a short line outside the theater to see On The Waterfront - that was their first date. They had first dropped Gary, who was seven then, off at the boy's grandmother's.

Their first date, yes, but had he met her briefly once before? Hadn't Vera, one evening, mentioned meeting a young nurse in the hospital cafeteria?

"Oh, she seems very nice, but she's got this crazy name - Lylah Peake!"

And yes, he had asked how she spelled her last name - was it p-e-a-k or P-e-e-k?

So Lylah had, in fact, met Vera at the hospital, and wasn't there a Christmas party some of the nurses organized that Vera and others on the secretarial staff were invited to attend? And hadn't Jerry and his wife gone?

Wait a minute- that's right- he had danced with her. He was drunk, of course, but he had danced with Lylah at the Christmas party. He recalled Vera dancing with Lylah's date, a rugged athletic type who'd rubbed Jerry the wrong way.

And it was while he was dancing with Lylah that she told him she had a rock from ancient Egypt - how in the world had that subject come up, anyway? Yes, it was all coming back to him now.

She had described the rock as having been passed down to her mother from a family relative, an aunt or cousin who had married an archaeologist in Manhattan a long time ago. It was funny- the things that came back to him once he opened that little door to the past. That odd little story had made an impression on him that night, but he felt certain he hadn't seen her again until their meeting in the supermarket a month or so after Vera's death, when she had placed her hand on the head of lettuce . . .

But now he was telling another nurse, presumably a good one - not one who might steal poison from the dispensary, that his little girl had just spoken. She hadn't opened her eyes or seemed to hear him, but she had -
" . . . Mumbled some incoherent words , words I couldn't quite understand."

"That's a good sign, Mr. Todd. Sometimes that's how they come back - in stages. Let's have a look."

The plump, sixty-ish woman, buzzing with surprising energy, took his elbow and propelled him ahead of her back down the hall toward Irene's room. A crash of thunder, blasting right above them, caused her hands to clasp both sides of her white stiff pointy cap.

"Oh, I would have to be on duty during this terrible storm! I could just murder my supervisor for changing my shift the way she did. We just heard on the radio that the Daltry Bridge is closed because of flash flooding."

When they came into the room, Irene was sitting bolt upright in the bed, both her little arms stretched out toward him.

"Daddy, is that woman Cousin Mildred? No, no, make her go away, make her go away! Her stone is all lit up, it's on fire!"

She collapsed back onto her pillow and seemed at once overtaken by sleep. The nurse felt her brow.

"Actually her temperature seems to be normal now, Mr. Todd. Try not to worry too much. She's what? Eleven?"

Jerry nodded his head.

"Difficult years for a young lady, yes they are," said the kind woman.

"You remind me of my mother, nurse. And I mean that as a compliment."

"Ah ,yes, I'll bet you were a regular mama's boy. I know the type."

Jerry smiled, his first one today.

"What's your name?"

Smiling, she pointed a chubby finger at her pin next to the white lapel of her tight-fitting uniform.

"Nurse Penny," she said.

"Worth lots more, I'll bet."

"Oh, yes," she replied, "a real mama's boy - I can spot them- always easy to fool."

Chapter 5: Five Minutes Later - The Todd House

Too much to deal with, that's all, too goddamned much. News that I've maybe three months to live- that's not bad enough. Irene's got another one of her seizures and I'm worried sick about her - being in that filthy hospital's brought all that crazy shit back from what is it, twelve years since I worked there? And this awful storm - I can hardly see the car in front of me through these relentless sheets of rain - wait, here's our street. And our umbrella's in the trunk, good place for it!

Lylah shut off the engine, grabbed her keychain from the ignition and bolted toward their front porch. Seconds later she stood in the dark but familiar living room, untying her soaked scarf. Tossing her jacket and purse on the coach, she bounded up the stairs without bothering to switch even a lamp on. No sooner was she in the upstairs hall than she saw a faint but distinct glow coming from their front bedroom.

A fire? Oh, for Christ's sake!

She pushed the half closed door open. The edges of her bottom dresser drawer were glowing- radiantly.

What the hell! Well, she HAD to open it.

27

She stooped, pulled the brass handle and gazed inside. The source of the light was the metal box she kept behind her panties- it held Mildred's stone. Before touching it, she turned and headed for the bathroom to get a glass of water. If it was a fire of some sort that had begun inside the bureau, she'd try to extinguish it. Think logically, Lylah, think logically.

How is it possible for a fire to start inside a drawer where there's nothing but my underwear and that ratty old box? Hot pants? That was supposed to be for boys.

Holding a plastic glass of water, she approached the dresser again, now seeing, thankfully, only darkness - reassuring, normal darkness. Had she imagined it? One of the nutty symptoms her tumor was producing? She placed the glass atop the bureau and sat down, exhausted, on the edge of their mattress. She stared at the stack of her silky white panties that looked like a gray blob in the shadowy dimness of the drawer's interior. Calm yourself, Lylah, calm yourself.

How long ago was it, that night Irene had stood right here at the foot of the bed?

"What is it, honey? Having a nightmare again?"

"Where do you keep Mildred's stone?"

Lylah remembered poking Jerry with her elbow and pushing their blanket aside to walk her back to her bedroom. Jerry didn't so much as stir behind her.

Cousin Mildred's stone had become her family's very own legend. Next to the stone inside the metal box was a folded time-worn newspaper article from January, 1923, as well as a few old letters and notes from people the woman had known in New York. There was also a report from an investigator her mother had hired to do a little family history investigation into the stone. She hadn't read this material in years. But she had showed the stone to Irene last year, allowing her to hold it in her hand for a while.

28

She told the girl some of the information about their long dead ancestor that might capture the imagination of a child. How Mildred herself was an heiress who lived in a luxurious house way up on Fifth Avenue back in the 1920's. That she fell in love with a young man who was studying Archaeology and, luckily, was hired by the Metropolitan Museum. Mildred's father was on the board of directors there and used his considerable influence to get his daughter's fiancée the position of curator in training, eventually overseeing the Egyptian Antiquities acquisitions.

"Here, Irene, you can see it, honey."

And they had played a little game with it, pretending it was a magic stone.

"Can I make a wish on it, Mommy?"

It had been a harmless game, surely. Lylah forgot what her daughter's wish had been. Wait, yes . . . now it came back to her.

Irene held the egg-shaped rock in her hand and said, "Be my friend forever, please."

********** **********

METROPOLITAN MUSEUM ANNOUNCES ANOTHER MAJOR FIND FROM ANCIENT EGYPT:

The city's major museum last night announced more valuable artifacts have been unearthed about two miles away from the Valley of the Kings in the Egyptian desert. The expedition, under the leadership of one of the museum's curators, Bernard Sheffield, has been digging and excavating there for nearly six months - finally bearing significant fruit in the past few weeks. The museum's spokesman, Kenneth Rundle, believes the descriptions he's received from Sheffield indicate the artifacts seem to be contents from "a very ancient temple."

When asked if the objects will equal the importance and value of the Tut treasures uncovered a few months ago by British archaeologist, Howard Carter, Rundle replied that "only time will tell." He did go on to say that a statue of the goddess Epronah must likely be at least 500 years older than the objects in Tut's tomb, because veneration of that deity was forbidden long before the boy-king's reign,

The new finds, currently being analyzed and catalogued, will probably not be shipped to New York for another few months. Meanwhile, citizens and lovers of all things Egyptian will just have to be content with picturing all the "beautiful things" Lord Carnarvon and Howard Carter brought home to London last November.

********** **********

The rain stopped, finally. How long had she been sitting on her bed in the darkened room? Feeling cold to the bone, she almost had to struggle to get up, then reached out to the open drawer. The quiet AFTER the storm can be just as creepy, she thought. Her trembling fingers quickly found the smooth, flat surface of the old metal box and pulled it out. Its dull, nearly black finish was cool to the touch, with no sign of a glow or even a shine to it now.

Then she sat back on the bed, noting, she thought, a sweet new odor in the air of the room. And she heard the faint sound of a stringed instrument being played - perhaps from a neighbor's house down the street. The Morgans had a son who played the violin - he was Irene's age. Luckily it wasn't the blasting music from the crazy Schusters, who bought a new stereo in the spring and forced everyone on the street to listen to their music - sometimes into the wee hours. This faint tune was, however, soothing.

Just when she began to open the box on her lap, she was overtaken by a sudden wave of dizziness that pushed her helplessly back onto the comfort of her bed. She closed her eyes, giving herself over to a restful, deserved nap, while the box, still unopened, lay on the bedspread next to her.

But no, it would not be that kind of sleep - more like a verbal assault from a harsh, judgmental presence, a voice she knew was a twisted version of her very own - a long dead twin in her brain- her tumor talking, perhaps?- and she tried, oh, how she tried desperately to wake up - but she couldn't. It was as though some sort of restraints had her fastened down, forcing her to listen to a stern lecture. Or perhaps more like a fairy tale, a bedtime story designed to produce nothing but anxiety and a nightmare.

Chapter 6 : The Nightmare

Like the worst ones, it began realistically. She found herself back in Rosemont Mercy Hospital, but this was about thirteen years ago. She was sitting in the cafeteria, across from the new girl recently hired in the billing department.

Her name was Vera Todd, a petite thing with short wavy hair and a cheerful smile. Lylah wondered what it might hide.

She'd always been suspicious of sweet tempered people - they instinctively drove her to want to crack that facade, for that is what it invariably was - a veneer of smiles and politeness for her to break through. She longed to get at the unpleasant nastiness under the surface. If she could arrange to have lunch with this Vera a couple of times in the cafeteria, she might pick up some clues about what she might really be like.

Lylah's mother, also a nurse, at a time when being a nurse meant something special, often used to tell her only daughter it was almost like being a nun. Ragged, jarring memories of her mother found their way into the dream. She remembered being given a book about Florence Nightingale as a child, sensing at an early age that her mother had a fixed vision of her little girl following in her footsteps. Only after she earned her own nursing degree did her mother allow her to start actively dating boys, with marriage as the next goal.

Mrs. Peake kept chiding her to stop driving each new boyfriend away. Lylah enjoyed mercilessly digging to find their faults, and then quickly send them packing.

"Pick, pick, pick - and they'll pick up and leave you, Lylah."

Her mother never guessed that marriage, at least in those early years, was the farthest thing from Lylah's mind. She simply liked the idea of chipping away at young men, until they came to resemble her preconceived notion of human nature: that everyone is the same - cheap and worthless.

And Lylah had always been pretty, never had a problem attracting young men. She found them, as a rule, generally stupid and remarkably easy to manipulate. She enjoyed what little power she was able to exercise over them just by pulling back from kisses or embraces that were too passionate. And she enjoyed, even knowing herself that this was odd, spoiling their exuberance or enthusiasm. It gave her a sense of control. She'd keep pushing them, needling them until they started withdrawing and finally stopped calling. Word finally got around, at least among her circle, that she was "a tease."

Eventually she realized she could get the same results from treating women, so-called friends, in the same way. But women were trickier, probably because her own good looks meant next to nothing to them. It wasn't as easy for her to get her foot in the door with girls - it just took a bit longer, forced her to work harder.

It was at nursing school where she found another outlet for her need to control. In her classes she sensed how totally she might be able to intimidate and supervise - not only her patients but her fellow nurses as well,particularly once she would start to rise through the ranks. So she held onto these thoughts, using them as the motivations to do exceptionally well in her studies.

Oh, there was always a great deal of talk about nursing being an opportunity to be of service and do good to humanity. Lylah had heard this line from her mother but saw all this as mere window-dressing, empty jargon that masked the underlying jewel: power.

And she was satisfied, when, after being on the staff at Rosemont Mercy for a few years, she felt sure of her abilities to regulate the routines of her patients' lives: making sure they took their pills, got their injections, submitted to her changing of their bandages . The myriad actions Nurse Lylah performed could be seen as services, certainly, but she viewed them as golden opportunities to take charge - if only briefly - of her patients' lives.

Then came that afternoon in the hospital cafeteria when, lunch tray in hand, she smiled sweetly at Vera Todd, recently hired as a secretary in the business office, and asked if she'd mind if she joined her at her table. The poor idiot returned a smile, delighted about the prospect.

The dream was allowing her back into the hospital cafeteria again. And right there, in that most ordinary lunch room setting, she experienced a truly momentous event. Vera had been talking on and on about her marvelous little boy and how her husband was so devoted to him. Then she took a pack of newly-developed photos from her yellow leather purse and slid it across the table toward Lylah.

"Just picked these up this morning. Have a look at them."

The one on top was of her husband holding his eight year old son high in the air, both of them grinning at the camera. Even the black and white tones revealed it was a sunny day on a beach somewhere, a typical vacation snapshot. But what was not typical was the glamour boy good looks of the husband, and the way his muscles revealed themselves in this pose - lifting the boy above him. Lylah was instantly reminded of her favorite movie star.

"My goodness, Vera, your husband looks like Tab Hunter !"

"Yes, he's handsome enough, I guess. I bought those swim trunks for him, and he almost didn't have the nerve to wear them."

Lylah had at once noted the way the white cloth stretched across his "generous endowment" - that was a phrase her mother had often used when she'd had too much to drink and began talking about men. Well, the phrase definitely applied to this man.

"Your son is cute as a button, Vera. What's your husband's name?"

"Jerry."

Lylah saw him in at least four other photos. In one of them, taken from above, he was lying on the sand, hands clasped behind his head and his eyes shut, while the boy seemed in the process of covering his chest with sand. Even asleep, or pretending to be, he was alive for Lylah in a way no other man had ever been. Then there was one, obviously meant to mock a body builder's strong man pose, in which he was flexing both biceps while little Gary straddled his broad shoulders. He had just enough dark hair visible on his chest and legs to draw attention to his masculinity - a nice contrast to his almost excessively pretty face.

She handed the photo pack back to Vera, who was still talking - though Lylah wasn't listening one bit to whatever she might be saying. Instead she was thinking only of Jerry, who, already in her mind, was becoming "her" Jerry. For she would have him - somehow.

It was only a matter of time.

A waiter in formal attire, white shirt and black bow tie, and having a shiny bald head, was suddenly at their table. Vera laughed out loud.

"What's he doing here, Lylah? This is a hospital cafeteria!"

"I can have him here if I want - this is my fucking nightmare!"

Vera's head of twisted curls was shaking now like an orb of tightly wound wires, her head trembling back and forth in a spasm of some kind.

"Please, Lylah," she was saying, "please don't do this!"

"Don't do what? Don't do what?"

"Waiter, can't you make her stop?"

Vera was screaming now, causing quite a scene. Lylah was embarassed. The nightmare was getting out of hand.

The waiter, very politely, asked Vera to leave. He stood behind her and gently pulled the chair out, helping her to stand.

"It's time, Vera, they need you back in the office," he reminded her.

Quick as a flash she was gone. Lylah was amazed to see he was suddenly growing hair from his shiny scalp as he took Vera's place across from her. The shape of his face began to change until he, too, began to resemble Tab Hunter.

"You have such a beautiful smile, Mr. Hunter," she said.

"Universal sent me to the best dentist in L.A." was his reply. "Now, what's this I hear about you planning to kill that poor young thing, Lylah?"

Chapter 7. The Nightmare, Part 2

She felt herself stir half awake, afraid to go any further in that direction just now. Could she possibly control the events of this awful dream, because she needed to sleep? Surely even a sleep like this was better than no sleep at all, wasn't it?

She was dancing now with the same waiter, bald again, not a trace of Tab anywhere. It was the Christmas party her nurse friends held, a Sunday night in early December. Lylah had arranged for some invitations to be sent to the secretarial staff, and Vera had arrived, as she had hoped, with her husband. The waiter gazed across the dance floor toward the entrance, and his face lit up.

"Your future boyfriend just arrived, honey bun."

Lylah's neck extended several inches in the designated direction. She saw him, no longer in a black and white photograph, but actually ten or twelve feet away. His eyes were casting around the crowded room, no doubt in search of table four. She herself had placed the white numbered cards on each table and had told Vera just this morning she and Jerry would be sitting next to her. Even more attractive in person, no other man at this affair would be able to rival him in handsomeness. Lylah felt a girlish flame of excitement deep inside.

The waiter nodded approvingly.

"Well, I do see what you see in him, Lye. And he's got lots of money. He may not make much money as a History teacher, but his wealthy old man just died a few months ago, and guess who got a huge inheritance? Vera is a lucky woman, yes indeed."

"Her luck is running out," said Lylah.

Shoving the waiter forcefully away from her in the middle of Petula Clarke's "Downtown," she headed for the new arrivals.

"I'll see you later, Lye!" she heard the waiter call from behind her. And she knew he was referring to a later segment of this awful dream she would have to endure before waking.

All she wished right now was to recapture, as accurately as possible, her first sight of Jerry. He and his wife had just hung their coats on the rack near the doors, and were a few feet away, looking for a familiar face. Vera let go of Jerry's hand when she spotted one of her secretary friends at a nearby table. This gave Lylah the chance to step forward and extend her own hand toward Jerry's.

"I think you must be Vera's husband. I'm Lylah Peake - Jerry, is it?"

His bright blue eyes flashed, the subdued amber lights overhead made his complexion shine, and he looked at her as though he were examining a rare and wonderful thing. The palm of his hand was dry and gripped her own with just the perfect combination of firmness and hesitation.

"Thanks for inviting us, Lylah."

That lovely, easy-going grin continued as he pointed his other hand down toward the shiny wooden floor.

"But tell me - why have you done this horrible thing?"

He wasn't smiling any longer.

She looked down, realizing the recording had halted and no dancers were swaying any longer to its rhythm. Couples stood stock still, all eying her with accusatory stares. An open casket was in the middle of the dance floor, and Vera, her eyes closed in death, was on display for all to see.

Her date, the bald waiter, stood above the casket and pointed a long slender finger at her.

"Yes, Lye, tell us!"

But a small drop of mercy fell from somewhere into this nightmare, and the recorded music began again. "The lights are much brighter there/You can forget all your troubles/Forget all your cares and go down town . . . down town."

Chapter 8 - Chip's Car - Ten minutes later

A half hour earlier they had pulled into a state store next to a gas station, and Gary had gone in, trying desperately to act one year older than he looked. His technique was to borrow Chip's wire rimmed glasses and, wearing them, walk slowly into the store - despite the buckets of rain pouring down.

It didn't take much effort to keep the young clerk from asking to see his I.D. Soon they were pulling back out onto the rain-soaked highway, mission accomplished.

Not driving now, Gary was working on his second beer; Chip, behind the wheel, and very much not trusting himself, had only a few sips of his first and handed the bottle to his friend. Wipers in overdrive, Chip was intent on getting them the rest of the way to Rosemont without any incidents. He asked himself when he was going to stop feeling like a high school kid and stop worrying so much. He remembered his dad telling him it was his mother's side of the family that was filled with worriers.

"It won't do me a damn bit of good to tell you to quit worrying about every little thing, Chip. It's just the way you are, and it's better than being like me, kid. I never worry about nothing - and I'm an ass hole - just ask anyone."

The rain increased its intensity the nearer they got to Rosemont. Chip mentioned that Gary's dad sounded like a pleasant enough guy on the phone - just to have something to say, because he sensed his friend's anxiety level was also on the rise the last few minutes.

"My dad's fine, I guess, but stepmother Lylah is a pain, let me tell you."

"Pain- how?"

"In addition to being a pain in the ass, she's a royal pain in the ass."

"Oh, now I understand completely, chum."

"I knew you would."

Gary opened the glove box and set the two beer bottles on its open door.

A yellow diamond shaped deer crossing sign flew by them. They were driving through the five miles or so of wilderness- wet wilderness tonight - just west of Gary's hometown. He wondered if he should spill some family business to Chip, then realized his friend knew no one even remotely connected to his family or anyone in Rosemont. Besides, the beer was doing its own good job of loosening up his inhibitions.

"See, the thing is I'm 95 percent sure she's cheating on my dad with this neighborhood guy."

"Wow . . . bummer, man. Are you sure?"

"At the end of the summer, I came home early one night when Dad was at a teachers' conference in Wilkes-Barre. I was in the kitchen raiding the fridge, you know, when I hear these heavy footsteps clunking downstairs. I call out, "Dad," but the front door closes real fast, and I bolt to the window to get a look at our front yard. And there's the back end of our neighbor from down the street- a guy who's a pretty good friend of my dad - named Bob Trekker. I recognized his goofy orange bowling shirt that's got his fucking last name printed all across his shoulders. I mean, can you imagine any guy being that stupid?"

41

"No other explanation for him hanging around?"

"So I holler up to Steppy - my nickname for her, by the way- 'what was Trekker doing here, Mom?' I choke on that word, but she's insisted I use it ever since she married Dad. And you know what her reply is?"

Chip was trying his best to hide his enjoyment of this tale.

"That he needed her to polish his bowling balls?"

"Funny, Chip, but not too far from the mark. She says she called him to fix a leak in the bathroom sink."

"A big fat lie, buddy."

"I'll drink to that," said Gary, reaching for his beer. "Can we find some music on this thing?" he asked, turning the radio on.

"Maybe you can find W-A-R-M," said Chip.

Gary fingered the dial til he hit the spot of their college town's popular channel and the gravelly-voiced announcer's voice.

" . . . listeners out there tonight on this rainy Thursday evening, here's our old pal Richard Harris with the very soothing and very long tribute to a rain-soaked MacArthur Park."

"Oh, fuck this shit," said Gary.

"Don't change it, dork!" yelled Chip, surprising even himself with his defiance.

"Well, since I suppose it is your car . . "

The hoarse rasp of the actor's troubled voice filled the car as it sped through the stormy night.

". . . Someone left the cake out in the rain\ I don't think that I can take it \ Cause it took so long to bake it/ And I know I'll never have the recipe again . . ."

The sudden appearance of a blanket of sopping wet fallen leaves on the black road in front of them was the first worrisome sign. Chip began to brake, but quickly saw branches, as well. He steered toward the right to avoid them. Then a length of a much longer branch, the width of a telephone pole, paid them a rude visit in the front seat as it smashed through the windshield.

Chapter 9 - The Todd House, 5 minutes Later

The green glow from the electric alarm clock on the bedside table lit up the hands at 8:05. The room was quiet, quiet and dark. The clock glowing, the metal box at her side - not. So maybe things were getting back to normal.

She would get her robe, change her clothes and throw some things in a bag before driving back to the hospital and her precious little girl. Then, almost as an afterthought, she flipped the lid of the box open. Knowing at once something was wrong, she couldn't figure, at first, what. The decades-old typed letter, the page ripped from an even older book - they were there. But the stone . . . It was there, but . . .
Lylah picked it up, held it close and turned the bedside table lamp on. No longer the size of a chicken's egg, it was now the size of a marble.

What was going on?

Still the same oval shape, with the odd vertical ridges resembling rows of corduroy cloth and the same two pointy triangles at the more narrow end. Just smaller - at least five times smaller.

Then she remembered the rays of light that had outlined the drawer a half hour ago.

"What have you been up to, you naughty little thing?"

Under it, the flesh of her palm detected a slight warmth, a life force? - Now what made that idea appear in her head? For an instant she wondered if she might still be dreaming, and she looked around the bedroom to get her bearings and maybe reassure herself. She saw their wedding picture on the opposite wall, hanging in the twilight like a ghost from the past.

Thirteen years ago she had posed for it as if it were the fulfillment of her life, which it was. The event for which she had given up so much - her decency- to achieve. Lylah, clenching her distant cousin's stone, not much more than a pebble now, walked round the bed to gaze more directly at the photograph. Especially at the groom.

That face, that smile, the sly twinkle in his eyes hinting at promises of sex for whoever might be lucky enough to be with him. Weeks after the wedding - no more than a mere month, she was already sensing him beginning to withdraw from her under the sheets. With that came the awful realization of the enormity of what she had done - dropped poison into Vera's coffee for a mere illusion of love. Stolen her husband because she had believed in his photogenic charms that had no doubt also seduced Vera herself six years before.

One hot summer night he was lying bare chested next to her and she let her fingers feel the bristly curled hairs around his nipples. Bending her head, she licked the one closest to her, tasting, she thought, a bit of salt and feeling the hardness of its tip. Groaning with what she hoped was pleasure in his half sleep, his legs shifted under the sheet. Surely, she thought, that was a signal for more, and she reached below to grab his penis. His response was to turn away from her.

"Oh, Lylah," he sighed, "give it a rest, will you?"

She remembered telling him - was it that night? - that a wife could divorce her husband for that.

"Yeah, but that would be a little drastic, wouldn't it?"

"Drastic, Jerry? You have no idea how far a girl can go - for love!"

"Honey pie, can't you learn to sort of settle for once a week? Some guys just don't have a big libido, I guess. I really can't help it. This is real life, baby, not a romantic movie. Now, let's go to sleep."

Yet from one of those rare contacts Irene, her darling baby, came to thrive inside her.

Snapping out of this unpleasant reverie, she pulled one of the closet's sliding doors open and made a grab for her red terry cloth robe. She saw her small overnight suitcase on the closet floor and began packing for the trip back to the hospital.

Suddenly, recalling the death sentence she'd received just hours before, she let out a bitter laugh. How could she have possibly buried that terrifying news for the past six hours? Its resurfacing made her literally collapse down onto the bed again.

She must have acquired a real talent for repressing nasty business over the years. She had done it before to her darkest deed, finally managing to almost erase it from her thoughts completely. The way she had gotten rid of Vera had made it much easier to forget.

It wasn't like she had pulled the trigger of a gun and blown her head off, or strangled her, or even pushed her over a cliff. There had been no physical contact at all. Nothing unpleasant for her to be forced to look at. Almost as though it hadn't really happened at all. And then she heard the talk about Vera's childhood heart ailment, which Lylah herself had read about weeks earlier when she snooped in the hospital's employee personnel files.

Lylah had finally managed to pull the whole thing together . . . it must have been about two months after Jerry had swept her away at that Christmas party.
In the hospital cafeteria, where she had been meeting Vera for lunch regularly, Lylah handed Jerry's wife a tube

of the new dark shade of pink lipstick Vera had complimented her on yesterday.

"Oh, thanks, Lylah. Let me pay you for it."

"Nonsense, Vera, but I'm dying to see how it looks on you."

"Let me go to the ladies' room and put it on."

Bingo, she was gone.

Lylah put a pinch of sugar on a coffee spoon, retrieved the small white envelope of digoxin from her purse and poured the grayish powder until she held a heaping teaspoon. With what she hoped was a natural gesture, she dipped it into Vera's cup, stirred it , being sure to add more sugar, then took it to the serving counter for a re-fill. When she returned to the table, Vera was just returning to their table.

"Here," said Lylah, "I got you a refill. Oh, I knew that shade would be perfect on you."

"I just hope Jerry will like it."

"Oh, men! Do they notice anything?"

They finished their lunch quickly, Lylah noting as she left the table that Vera had drained her cup.

Forty-five minutes later the elevator in the lobby opened, and a doctor discovered Vera on the floor, twitching, with a trickle of foam dripping down her chin from her "coral pink" lips.

Lifted onto a gurney and rushed to the emergency room, Jerry's wife was dead by the time she got there.

********** ***** **********

Lylah relaxed her clenched fist and looked at what remained of her family heirloom in her palm. Matter is not destroyed, it undergoes a transformation - hadn't she come across this idea years ago in a science textbook or a lecture? Could there actually be something like that going on here? But why now, why tonight?

Her child had held the stone in her hand for the first time - when was it? - last year, yes. And Lylah hadn't looked at it again until tonight, when she had "seen the light" as they say. When exactly might it have begun to shrink in size? And what had become of the lost, or transformed, part of it?

And then it dawned on her.

Energy. Irene's recently-discovered new powers had to have been triggered by something: this exotic rock from Ancient Egypt? Why not?

Irene had asked it to be her friend.

She felt a faint throbbing in her forehead, the unmistakable precursor to one of her familiar headaches.

Wait a minute.

Wait just one minute.

When had her headaches begun? Weeks, perhaps no more than two months, after she showed Irene the stone.

Doctor Barrow had given Irene an X-ray of her brain just hours ago. He would see the results of it in the morning and then talk to both of them in the hospital.

Tumors. Two of them? One giving power, one taking power away.

This must be exactly what madness is like, she thought, as she stifled a scream with her knuckles and backed away from the bed. The shrunken stone lay on the spread, where she'd placed it next to the open metal box, its interior drawing her in, as if toward a pit.

Chapter 10: Contents of the Pit

The typing at the top of the paper identified the writer as Clarence Sternov, staff researcher for Family Heritage Tracing Services in Brooklyn. It was addressed to her mother,Catherine, thirty years ago. Lylah was reading it now for the first time since she was sixteen:

*** . ********** . *** . ********** . ***

Mrs. Peake,

Your cousin Mildred was the only child of Adam and Diana Windgate. Her father's fortune, though nowhere near the wealth of the Vanderbilts or Rockefellers, was large enough to move him and his first wife into nearly the highest echelons of New York City's aristocracy in the early years of this century. Adam acquired his riches through purchasing twenty acres of forest land in Northern California in 1871, and then, with the kind of immense good luck that is the stuff of legend; and the physical strength of three good friends who knew how to use picks, axes and mules, discovered- what else? - gold.

Adam then moved, with his wife and their three amply-rewarded friends, back east. The Windgate House was eventually built up on the northern reaches of Fifth Avenue on a lot that would soon be a very populated section of 91st Street. Adam, age twenty-nine when the House was built, over the next five years would endure the deaths of his infant son and,months later, that of his wife. Wasting little time grieving, within three months he had married again - this time his housekeeper, Diana Malone. They would have only one child, a daughter named Mildred, born in 1899 in the great house on East 91st Street. A baby brother, born the next year, lived only a few months, leading to little Mildred becoming, as the years passed, an heiress.

By 1920 she had had her "coming out" debut in society and was living at home with only her still vigorous mother for company; her father having died two years before due to a heart attack while strolling through Central Park. A live-in housekeeper/cook named Sarah , and a man servant who doubled as a chauffeur, also resided there.

In the spring of that year Mildred met and quickly fell in love with Bernard Sheffield, a curator at the museum just down the avenue from her house. She found him to be both scholarly and athletic, qualities she felt were rarely seen in combination. Bernard saw in her only her kind nature and curvaceous figure; and an ability to seem, at least, interested in his comments and conversations about museum matters.

Her father, just before his death, made a huge bequest to the museum to finance an archaeological expedition to Egypt to excavate a parcel of desert rumored to be the location of a very old tomb. Mr. Windgate had always wanted to visit Egypt and thought this would be an excellent opportunity to be both tourist and head of a philanthropic enterprise. Plans for this very project had just begun when his heart stopped beating in the Park that day. A few weeks after his funeral, Mildred visited the museum and expressed her wish to continue her father's endeavors regarding "the dig." She was introduced to some officials, one of whom was Bernard Sheffield, the new curator of Egyptian antiquities.

A little over two years later, upstaged and out-publicized by the Tut discoveries, Bernard saw his own unearthed artifacts were weakly promoted and mostly relegated to storage containers in the museum's cellars - for "possible exhibition at some time in the future." He did, however, keep one small item as a memento for his darling Mildred, the little carved stone that was the first object the diggers found - just a few feet from the exact spot Mildred had suggested they begin digging.

For your cousin Mildred, you see, had gone to Egypt with Mr. Sheffield, who by then was her fiancée. It was she, he claimed, after months of fruitless digging, suggested they try digging "over there by those strange looking rocks." After less than an hour of surface digging, the workers began to see the unmistakable level surface of first one stair, then another - until finally revealing what eventually came to be known as the temple of Epronah.

Someone at the museum, at our agency's request, found an old textbook that contains rather limited information on this obscure deity, although you will see(when you read the enclosed materials that are the primary sources for our information) there is some question as to whether this female personage was, in fact, even a goddess at all - or something else entirely.

Mildred and the curator did marry, their union producing one child, a son also named Bernard. When the boy was six or seven, the Stock Market collapsed and the Windgate fortune suffered a similar fall. Mildred's poor husband, it seems, took his own life by leaping from a high window ledge of the Astor Hotel in 1930. A few months later mother and son boarded a train west to live with Adam's niece in a little town called German Falls, Wisconsin.

It was there that young Bernard formed a close attachment to a young cousin named Catherine, whose father was a farmer named John Kanner. He is, I believe, your father, Mrs. Peake. Your cousin Bernard gave you that odd little stone as a gift just before you left your father's farm in Wisconsin to come east to live with your older sister in Baltimore.

Bernard was killed in action during the war in the battle of Guadalcanal. Shortly after you left, Mildred passed away (she is buried in the German Falls Cemetery) and had always said it would be best to keep the "temple stone" in close proximity to women.

It seems there is a legend that Epronah's followers were exclusively female. From your photograph and description of the item, I would say it just might have significant value as an antique and would be a fine heirloom to keep and pass on to posterity.

This is all the information we have been able to glean due to the minimal fee you provided. Should you wish to search for more detailed facts concerning your family ancestry, do not hesitate to contact our agency again.
***** . ***** . *****

The paper under this letter had a ragged edge on its left side, as though Clarence, or one of his researchers, had ripped it from a book, perhaps some sort of encyclopedia. Lylah , sitting on the edge of the bed, inched a little closer to the lamp to read it, noting the rain had started up again.

EPRONAH - goddess worshipped by a relatively small but aristocratic group of women followers during the Early Dynastic Period around 2900B.C. in Memphis. Rituals to her have been traced back as far as the time of King Menes, the earliest of known Egyptian rulers, and founder of the so-called Old Kingdom. Hieroglyphic panels suggest her identity changed considerably with the passage of time , her earliest images depicting her as a malign , nearly demonic force.

At some point it became unlawful to worship Epronah, and her followers were forced to disband and conduct their rituals underground in secret tunnels. During these years her identity seems to have been recreated into a spirit having the power to destroy or punish anyone who had committed wicked deeds. Toward the end of the period known as the Old Kingdom, she was commonly known as "the punisher," a figure of near heroic dimensions. Her acolytes believed Epronah's presence was felt in certain rock formations of the earth, and carved stones were no doubt used in their temple services.

***** ********** *****

Someone from the agency had circled this final sentence with a flourish of red crayon in order, no doubt , for Lylah's mother to make the connection to her family's stone. The artifact may have survived the long centuries of time on this planet, but under Lylah's stewardship it had been reduced to a shrunken pebble.

A few other papers remained in the box, letters and jottings with information regarding the agency's sources in Manhattan and Wisconsin for the biographical material in the official report.

Lylah, by this time, had had enough.

A flash of white lightning suddenly lit the bedroom, followed instantly by a deafening blast of thunder cracking above the house. Jumping to her feet, she felt her hand stabbing with pain as if it were on fire - had she been electrocuted? She'd forgotten she'd been holding the stone while reading the material. Her fingers - were they her fingers? - they looked darker and strangely wrinkled in the flashes from the lightning. They held what was left of the stone, close to her burning palm. Dropping it now onto the carpet, she saw it lay smoking at her feet. Fearful of a house fire, she stomped it with her shoes, then turned to get the glass of water she hadn't needed earlier from her bureau. She emptied it onto the smoldering, ashy remnants of her heirloom.

Suddenly she breathed in the fragrance of hundreds of flowers, as though she'd been magically transported to a botanical garden exhibit. She felt on the verge of fainting, in a feverish swoon, seemingly transported to another time, another place.

Knowing she was experiencing a special moment, a deep revelation of some kind, she had to sit, just for a minute or so, on the bed. She must collect her thoughts, and it crossed her mind that this must be what the hippies meant by the hallucinatory effects of LSD - an altered state of consciousness. Hearing the same stringed instrument she'd heard before, only louder, she shook her head repeatedly, trying to make it stop. Then she was startled to hear a chorus of women's voices somewhere nearby, intoning a mournful hymn. It was as though they were in the next room, chanting.

Perhaps a new Lylah was being born.

After a minute or so, her exhaustion having yielded to a kind of determination, she felt herself drawn back to the bedroom closet. She knew, instinctively, what she needed most - the yellow cardboard box she hadn't opened since her last day of working at Rosemont Mercy. She would pack it with the other items she'd need to spend the night at the hospital. . . at the bedside of her sweet Irene.

Chapter 11: The Hospital - 15 Minutes Later

Jerry stood at the window, looking out across the parking lot, and saw the rows of wet car tops and pavement shining under the lights. Another assault of rain was lashing across the town. An ambulance, its solitary red roof light glowing like a moving ball of lava, coasted toward the emergency entrance nine stories below. He looked back at his daughter, who was now, thankfully, sleeping- and wished he could do the same.

Even if she were to instantly snap out of it and recover from whatever strange emotional issues held her in their grip tonight, Jerry knew his life would never be the same. Minutes ago she had told him, with many more details, and still mimicking Lylah's identical voice, about what had happened to Vera. That voice was carved in his brain now like a flame-hot brand from a cowboy's strong arm.

"I spooned the digoxin in her coffee, and I did it so I could have Jerry. He danced with me at the Christmas party, he held me close - the way a man does when he wants a girl to actually feel his strength, you know? I knew then he would be mine. All I needed to do was get that silly, dim-witted wife of his out of the way."

It was hard for him to listen to this, especially from his lovely, innocent little girl.

There were bitter things he worried about as he stood at the streaked window, hands in his pockets - a stance Lylah always referred to as his "anxiety posture."

"We always know trouble is brewing when Jerry stands like that."

One troubling concern, the most fraught with worry, was that his little girl would need to be committed to a psychiatric facility for observation and care.   And how long might that go on? If her ramblings and provocative accusations became evident to Dr. Barrow tomorrow, he might at once recommend such action.

Also of uppermost concern was how to inform Lylah of the horrifying accusations her daughter was making against her. She would no doubt be here soon, and he would have to confront her.

Had he been living with a killer all these years? Would he have the courage to ask her?

But Barrow himself had said Vera had died of a heart attack - as well as the coroner. While it was true she was only thirty-five, her parents were quick to recall she'd been diagnosed during infancy with a heart problem they referred to as a "murmur."

They'd taken her for yearly electrocardiograms, her doctors noting steady improvements as the years passed. Sometime when Vera was in high school, the family moved and changed doctors. Her robust good health led them to gradually ignore this unpleasant past diagnosis and assume it had been eradicated.

Her parents' tearful acknowledgment of their negligence was what led Dr. Barrow to rule her death to have been due to a heart attack. Vera had exhibited all the symptoms of sudden cardiac arrest to the doctors in the emergency room at Rosemont Mercy as well.

But Lylah had been a nurse, a good one, and it was logical that she might have learned a thing or two about poisons. Drugs and poisons were no doubt easy for her to have access to here at the hospital. Irene had used the word "dispensary." Could Lylah also have learned about Vera's past heart issues?

One thing that had attracted Jerry to Lylah from the start was her self-confidence. Perhaps she felt he would be easy for her to manipulate, once he was free to marry again.

Lylah would be here soon, and Jerry couldn't help but see his life was coming full circle tonight, bringing him back to this god-awful place. . . for what purpose he had no idea.

Jerry had spent a good chunk of his life teaching History at Rosemont High School, yet here he was, struck by the knowledge that he had been ignorant of the dark truth behind his own personal history for the past thirteen years.

Then, in a blurred reflection in the rainy window glass, he saw the figure of Lylah behind him in the doorway. He turned to face her, as she placed her overnight bag and a rather large yellow cardboard box on the floor next to the bed. Without saying a word to him, she felt Irene's forehead and kissed it.

"She doesn't have a fever. Has she spoken anything yet?"

"Yes,Lylah, but it didn't sound like her."

"What do you mean, Jerry?"

"She sounded like you. If my eyes had been closed, I would have sworn her voice was yours."

Lylah cocked her head, quizzically.

He noticed she had a small bandage wrapped around her hand.

"What's happened to your hand?"

"It's complicated. I'll tell you about it later."

"That's how you deal with things, is it?"

"I don't understand. What did she say?"

He approached her, put his hand on her shoulder and drew her back toward the window. He lowered his voice to a whisper.

56

"It was like a confession, what she said. And she used words, expressions she can't possibly be familiar with."

"Like what?"

"Like 'dispensary' and 'digoxin'. "

She spun around like a top, and in a flash he was looking at the back of her head, her hair hanging like a dark curtain. She raised her hand to shoulder level, shaking her wrist like a student needing to go to the lav. But he recognized it as a plea for silence.

"You can't face me, can you? Is that your answer then? You DID it, you killed Vera?"

Placing both hands on her shoulders, he turned her to face him, but she kept her eyes focused on the floor.

"I must have been out of my mind in those days. One look at you in those snapshots she brought out to show off that day - and I was lost. Never felt that strongly about anyone before. Does that make you feel smug? Does it build up your ego to know how far this sad, pathetic woman went to get you, Jerry?"

"Smug! Want to know how I feel? Try 'played for a sucker' baby - that's how I feel!

I thought we had a marriage, Lylah - instead I guess it's been more like a trap - for me anyway. Only it took me thirteen years to find out I'd been roped and thrown in a cage."

She lifted her head a bit and poked his chest, wanting to get them as far away from their sleeping child as possible. She kept her voice low, and to Jerry it began to sound raspy, almost like a growl. She managed to back him into the farthest corner of the small room.

"And it took me about one month to find out what a cold fish you were, how dull you were- maybe you and Vera were made for each other!"

"I guess maybe we were. And you put an end to that."

She lifted her head and looked him square in the face, distant thunder a reminder that this awful weather was still prowling through the skies above Rosemont.

"Well, I got my punishment today. Can you hang in there for a few more months and let nature run its course?"

"I don't know. From now on, am I an accessory or something? I don't know. Shouldn't I see a lawyer? Or shouldn't you?"

"If I went to one tonight, I might just say we planned it together - don't put it past me."

It was his turn now to turn his back on her. He went over to his daughter's bedside. In the shadows from the weak covered bulb on the wall above her sleeping face, she looked like one of the many dolls they had bought her over the years, until about two years ago, when she stopped being interested in dolls. What were her new interests? Would he ever understand anyone - even his own children?

For some reason, he had a vision of Gary, "Vera's boy," as he began to think of him not long after her death. Nothing of Lylah, thankfully, in his son. The habit the boy had of staring up at the ceiling or sky before saying something important- just as Vera had always done. Or how he would pause between certain words in conversation to emphasize them: "Listen . . . to . . . me." Or the habit he'd acquired of rubbing the back of his neck when he was stressed. Even his eyes, the look Jerry would get from him occasionally in the boy's sly, knowing glances.
Vera's.

He heard a rustle of clothing behind him and saw Lylah taking off her jacket. There was a narrow closet near the door where she headed to hang it up. Then she came over and stood behind him.

"How can she know these things?" she finally asked, and he felt the pressure of her breasts against his back.

"I was hoping," he said, "you'd say she was making it up."

58

"You never said anything to Gary about Vera's death being suspicious? Could he have said something to Irene?"

"Lylah, I didn't even have suspicions myself. I know you and Gary never see eye to eye about anything, but - murder - no, never. Neither of us ever would have imagined that. Look, let's go down the hall - away from her for a while."

They walked down the corridor, passing a few patients' rooms toward an alcove where several vacant cushioned chairs were positioned across from the elevator. Jerry sat down first, Lylah lit a cigarette and began pacing. From somewhere nearby they heard women's voices, presumably nurses, talking quietly. No doubt they were at their station, a little farther down the hall. An announcer's radio voice, muffled by static, was giving an update on the weather alerts.

Jerry asked her to sit down, and after taking a few brief steps back and forth past the elevator doors, she did, next to the standing metal ash tray at his side.

"What are we going to do?" he asked.

"You're going to go home and wait for Gary. In the morning you can bring him here to see Irene. We can have breakfast in the cafeteria and wait for Dr. Barrow."

Something like a bitter, mocking laugh was about to come out of his mouth, but he stifled it.

"And when should I tell him you murdered his mother?"

She leaned toward him across the ash tray, exhaled a stream of smoke, glaring at him.

Her reply was soft, almost a hiss.

"I don't give a fuck, Jerry."

She stubbed the butt in the round amber glass tray and started to get up. He gestured toward her, and it surprised him that she abruptly halted.

"Lylah, a few hours ago we saw our little girl in Dr. Barrow's ceiling lamp, and just now she was imitating

your voice, telling me you poisoned Vera with digoxin " -
He was on his feet now, next to her but still fighting to
keep his voice down.

"And where exactly is this "dispensary" any how?" he
asked.

Both on their feet now, she jerked her head a bit
toward the left.

"Just down the hall, and I'll bet they still don't keep it
locked. Oh, stop acting like a wounded animal! If you only
knew what I've had to deal with back at the house - let
alone with Barrow's news this afternoon -"

"The house, what happened at the house?"

She told him everything then, or at least most of it.
She'd told him years ago about the peculiar stone her
mother had given her as an heirloom, and she knew he
had once read through the papers under it. But now she
added tonight's chapter, maybe the final chapter, in the
Egyptian rock's story: the light coming from the drawer,
her theory about the possibility that the stone's energy
had caused Irene's powers as well as her own tumor.

"This is," she added, "said to be a powerful, vengeful
goddess or spirit - according to a history book, Jerry, -
that's supposed to be your field, isn't it, Mr. History
teacher? Stop looking at me that way!"

Her rant had worn him out, tired him, forcing him
finally back down onto the cushioned chair. He asked her
for a cigarette, and she sat down again as well.

"Are you sure," he asked, gazing around, "this place
isn't a nut house? - because that's where I think this kind
of talk might fit."

The elevator door across from them opened, and the
nurse Jerry had met earlier got off. She looked inquiringly
at Lylah, who smiled up at her.

"Nurse Penny," she said, standing up to extend a
hand, adding, "it's Lylah Peake, but now Mrs. Todd.
Remember me?"

"Hard to forget you, dear."

Jerry was standing now too, and told Lylah he'd met Nurse Penny earlier.

"She and I used to work together here years ago, Jerry. Grace was practically my mentor here."

"You haven't changed much, Lylah. I'm sorry to see your little girl here."

"We're hoping Dr. Barrow will give us some good news in the morning, aren't we, sweet heart?"

"She seems a bit better now, and my wife got it cleared to spend the night in her room."

Oh, my," said Nurse Penny, "dear, dear, that's right - " and a troubled expression crossed her face.

"What is it?" asked Jerry.

"They've just had an admission down at the emergency room, and I think I heard someone mention the name Todd - I did think it sounded familiar. Could it be a relative?"

He shot a look of panic at Lylah.

"Gary - he's driving in this storm."

Jerry reached out to press the elevator button. It opened immediately. He asked Lylah to stay with Irene, telling her he'd come up and let her know if it was their son as soon as he knew. As the doors closed, he heard Nurse Penny tell Lylah to come with her to the nurses' station.

Chapter 12: Ceremony of the Night Wind - A Few Minutes Later

The man's voice over the radio sounded as if it were broadcasting from a tunnel, an echo vibrating after every few words: "Extremely high gusts are expected with these final bands of rain sweeping across the area. Residents of Scranton , Honesdale and as far north as Rosemont and Binghamton are advised to stay indoors for the next few hours, as winds nearing tornado force are expected to have the potential to cause considerable damage. Local municipalities are concerned about the possibilities of flooding, as creeks rise. Power failures have already been reported . . ."

His voice trailed off until finally she heard a soothing familiar voice - was it Jo Stafford ?-singing one of the great old songs from the 1950's. The singer deserved better accompaniment than the scratchy static she was getting tonight ,though, that was for sure.

"See the pyramids along the Nile/ Watch the sun rise on a tropic isle/ Just remember, darling, all the while/ You belong to me ."

Lylah drew the curtains closed across the window, saw Irene still lost in a sleep of some sort, and then quietly closed the door. She lifted the yellow box she'd brought from home and placed it on the bed, at the girl's feet. Across its top were emblazoned the words, Fowler, Dick and Walker, The Boston Store. She opened it, hearing at once the rustle of the tissue paper she'd used to protect the contents thirteen years ago, a few days before her wedding. Her white nurse's uniform and cap, its points and stiff starched edging outlined in blue, stared up at her. She'd packed her white slippers into the traveling bag, along with her identification pin with the two words "Nurse Peake" in black against a pale green background. Lylah remembered paying an engraver ten dollars to get it done precisely the way she wanted. She retrieved the shoes and pin now from the bag and began to undress, down to her silk slip.

Just underneath her folded white dress in the box, lay the bright blue nurse's cape that had been part of her mother's nursing uniform. Lylah recalled wearing it a few times when she was first hired at Rosemont Mercy. She enjoyed the way she looked in it, even more the almost regal feeling it gave her. She'd never forgotten Nurse Penny's comment in those early years.

"Those of us who have a flare for the dramatic usually like to wear them in public, but I don't need to draw attention to myself that way, Lylah. It's much too bold a fashion statement, but then - that's you, isn't it? Bold."

Good old Penny had hit the nail right on the head then and there. Bold, dramatic - perhaps performing on stage would have been a better career for her to pursue: an actress, able to hold audiences in the palm of her hands for a couple of hours every night. Maybe she'd get another chance in her next life, but this one, as she'd been told today - this one was nearly over.

Still, she would at least have tonight.

Lylah had tasted power as a nurse in those long ago days. She recalled how most of her patients' eyes lit up when she arrived with her convincing smile and carefully rehearsed words of concern. They would allow her to give them injections, wash them in their most intimate places and swallow their prescribed pills. All the while, though, she knew something was missing - she wanted to do more.

Vera had come along with her bright eyes, displaying those photos of her perfect husband and his loving son. How wonderful it might be to have power over them. Taking the poison from the dispensary and using it for the desired effect would lead her, inevitably, into the arms of a beautiful man. And she just knew by his kindly, charming ways he'd be a cinch to control - and later their children, too. But married life had turned out to be a trap, one she hadn't expected.

Jerry - Mr. Ice - a male version of those beautiful but coldly frigid women psychologists like to analyze and write about so much.

So that today, when Barrow gave her the awful news, she figured it was over. The end of any chance she'd ever have of continuing any measure of control over her own life, let alone anyone else's. Death was suddenly coming for her, exerting its own ultimate power. Then, incredibly, the odd little stone had come to her rescue in a very strange and complex way today, bringing first her daughter - here - to Rosemont Mercy, and now herself. She felt she was on familiar turf again. Home, sort of.

Listening to the rushing wind behind the closed curtains, she put her old uniform on in a flash. Because she hadn't gained one pound in thirteen years, it still fit. She pinned the identification pin just above her left breast, and fastened her cap onto her hair with two bobbi pins. Then she pulled the cape up out of the box and with, yes - a dramatic - flourish, swept it around her shoulders and turned to gaze at her reflection in the wide mirror on the wall behind her.

Nurse Lylah was ready to make her rounds. The dispensary was just down the hall, and patients were waiting for her on the top floor, in the critical care ward.

She turned and noted a distinct fluttering of the drawn curtains. Despite the tightly closed windows, little drafts of air had found their way through old bricks and wooden frames to breathe into the room. Nature was putting on

64

quite a display tonight. Lylah was invigorated, and stood before the slightly trembling long curtains like a figure from scripture before a holy place. She felt at one with the elements, united to their power, if only for a few more hours.

Without so much as a glance at the figure on the bed next to her, she turned and left the room. Corridor lights had always been dimmed after 9 o'clock, and she was happy to see the tradition continued. Beginning to walk down the dimly lit hall, she saw a young nurse, helping a man wearing a robe, coming toward her. They both stared at her, surprised no doubt by the cape she wore.

Using an authoritarian tone she found surprisingly easy to dredge up, she asked the girl if the dispensary was still down the hall on the right.

"Why, yes, ma'am - it is. Do you have a key?"

Luckily, Lylah had carefully crafted a cover story for her presence in the building.

"No, I don't. I'm the substitute private duty nurse for a patient down on the fifth floor. I didn't expect it to be locked."

The young nurse introduced herself as Debbie Nelson.

Lylah leveled a radiant smile at the patient, who, although somewhat unsteady on his feet, used the cane expertly.

"If you could spare your lovely escort for a minute, perhaps she could let me into the dispensary?"

They both smiled at her. The nurse left her patient, took her keys from her pocket and followed Lylah down the hall.

It was that easy.

"I love your cape. We're not required to have them here. I've only seen them on posters."

"My mother was a nurse, so it was hers. This is such a terrible night, and I know how chilly these old hospital buildings get - good reason to wear it."

"That's why I simply wear one of my sweaters, ma'am."

Bitch, thought Lylah.

Outside, the wind seemed to be picking up its intensity.

***** . ***** . ***** . *****

Blondie, after telling her to remember to turn the latch on the inside of the door before leaving, didn't bother waiting for Lylah to finish her errand. Instead, eager to return to her patient, she left Lylah alone inside the dispensary.

One flick of the light switch revealed the recent remodeling and layout of the room: new blue linoleum flooring ,vertical strips of yellowish-brown paneling and rows of glass cases with sliding doors. Considerable changes since her time, but still mostly a disorganized mess. She began by searching the cabinets in the closest aisle for the morphine. While thus engaged, she took a plastic tray from a nearby table, as well as a syringe from a drawer labeled "injection supplies."

Behind her, the door slowly opened. Nurse Penny was genuinely startled to see the caped figure, bent over, at the far end of the aisle.

"Excuse me, Nurse Debbie told me someone might need some assistance?"

Lylah had stooped to get something from a bottom shelf but straightened up and turned to face her intruder.

A pained grimace crossed the older nurse's face when she saw it was Mrs. Todd, attired in her uniform and that relic of a cape.

She headed down the narrow aisle between the cabinets toward Lylah.

"Really, my dear, you have no right to be here. You should be in your daughter's room. That was the agreement Dr. Barrow arranged with us. You're no longer employed here."

Lylah drew her arm back, then thrust it forward quickly, jabbing the surgical scissors once, twice, three times into Penny's mid-section. With the final strike, she plunged deep, then startled even herself by grasping the woman's shoulder with her free hand, holding it down for leverage, and lifted her other hand, that held the scissors, upward in order to do more serious damage. Dull terror in her eyes, the victim never made a sound, as splotches of blood seeped into the white fabric of her dress, and she crumpled to the floor.

How much of the howling was from the wind outside, and how much was shrieking in her own head, Lylah couldn't judge. She only knew she still had much to do. It only took her another minute or two to locate the little glass vials of morphine and place them on the tray next to the syringe. Taking a wide step over Penny's heap, she headed for the partially open door, flicked off the light, turned the latch and locked the door behind her.

Patients were waiting for her on the floor above.

An ear-piercing crack of thunder seemed to explode just above the building's roof. Suddenly the lights shut off across the entire floor. The startled screams of women, no doubt nurses as well as patients, echoed in the darkness. Lylah stood frozen in place, leaning against the wall, still not far from the dispensary. She held the tray steady, sighing with relief when the lights quickly flashed back on.

But at the far end of the corridor, near the alcove that held the elevator, she saw a familiar small figure wearing a patient's gown.

***** ***** ***** *****

Downstairs on the main floor, the emergency room lights also went out as the blast of thunder roared.

Dr. Barrow was so startled he dropped the patient's chart.

67

"Jesus Christ," said Jerry, standing next to him, "that must have hit something nearby."

As quickly as they had gone out, all the lights came back on. The cluster of doctors, orderlies and nurses in the area gave welcome sighs of relief.

Barrow re-iterated how fortunate Gary had been to have survived with only a couple of bruises.

"You poor devil, your entire family is here tonight."

His son's room mate hadn't been as lucky, but would no doubt be "right as rain" in a few days, having suffered a broken leg, with no signs of internal injuries. The car, though, was a total loss.

Gary was right there, sitting up on the edge of a gurney, feeling awkward wearing only an open backed hospital gown.

"Can't I get my clothes back, Doc?"

"I'm afraid they're soaked, Gary. Your dad can drive home and get you a change of clothes. Why don't you go down the hall and talk to your buddy - you know, from what I hear, he saved your life."

No sooner had Gary stood up than Jerry put his arms around him and held him close.

"Gee, Dad, you haven't hugged me so much since I was six."

Jerry watched as his son walked down the hall to Chip's gurney, chuckling at the sight of the boy's hand trying in vain to keep the back of his gown closed.

Barrow suggested Jerry go up to tell Lylah the good news.

"First I want to thank that Chip again. Is someone phoning the kid's parents?"

"Yeah, we'll notify the parents. Try and relax. You and your family have had a trying day."

"That's the truth, Doc."

Jerry walked away to join his son at Chip's side, thinking he'd take the elevator up to see Lylah in a few minutes.

***** . ***** . ***** . ***** .

Surely that was Irene standing down there in the shadows, but when Lylah heard the child begin calling out, the voice was husky, not her daughter's but some other, older voice. Hadn't Jerry mentioned something about her voice sounding different?

"Lylah!" called the strange voice, "Lylah!"

And why, she wondered, is she using my first name? It must be due to the sedative she was given earlier. She placed the tray carefully down on a nearby window sill and headed down the corridor toward the child. The lights flickered off and on, and when she looked again, Irene had vanished. Ducked around the corner near the elevator, no doubt. Lylah heard footsteps behind her and turned to see Blondie at the opposite end of the shadowy hall.

"Did Nurse Penny see you, ma'am?"

"Yes, honey, everything's fine."

Lylah hurried now, her cape swirling as she dashed around the corner into the alcove. And there was her darling Irene, looking very much like her old self, her little hand holding the elevator door open.

"Come on, Lylah - " but she was continuing to use that ridiculous voice. "Oh, hurry, we'll go down together!"

Irene disappeared inside the elevator,

Lylah swooped in behind her ,and at once screamed, falling straight down into the awful darkness until she hit the hard roof of the motionless car on the ground floor.

An eerie silence settled over the ninth floor for about thirty seconds. Finally, distant footsteps could be heard running up a stairwell, growing louder as the runner drew closer to this floor. A door opened nearby and soon Jerry's voice was heard asking where his wife and daughter were.

In a few seconds he and Nurse Debbie were coming to check the alcove.

"I did see," said the nurse,, "what looked like a little girl around here, but that strange new nurse with the cape - she was around here, too."

They walked slowly toward the gaping doorway.

"Oh, my goodness, sir - be careful. There must have been some sort of a power failure. This is a real hazard - maybe we should drag one of these chairs in front of the opening so no one falls through."

A male orderly came up to them to report that a couple of patients claimed to have heard a scream.

"Mister," the attendant said to Jerry, "are you all right?"

Seeing he was visibly trembling, the man approached him.

"My daughter - could she have - ?"

Jerry turned, facing the wall of darkness that stretched before him, and held both sides of the elevator doors with the tight pressure of his hands. He stared down into the abyss.

"Irene!"

His echo drifted back, faint but as mournful as the original.

Then a sort of scraping movement from just above his head caused him to look up. Clinging to a ridge in the shaft wall about three feet above his head, his little girl was, incredibly, lowering herself toward his outstretched hands. The orderly put his arms around Jerry's chest to steady the guy, whose feet were right on the edge of the drop.

The young nurse looked in wonder as the girl's little bare legs slipped easily into her father's grasp. Jerry then carried her over to one of the two leather chairs.

"Oh, baby, how did you get up there?" he asked.

"I think I flew," she replied in her familiar, clear child's voice.

Chapter 13 - Ground Floor - 5 minutes later

Jerry carried Irene down the nine flights of stairs to the lobby, Nurse Debbie just behind them. He would surely meet up with Lylah down there somewhere. Though eager to tell her the good news about Gary, he still knew they would have to iron out the issues concerning what she had confessed about Vera's death.

Neither of them knew a criminal lawyer, and he simply didn't know in what sort of jeopardy he himself might be in if he neglected to do anything. Right now all he could think about was savoring every precious moment of holding Irene close to his shoulder, as they carefully descended the poorly lit stairs. Recalling the child's words, "I think I flew, Daddy," he wondered for a second just who or what it was he was holding in his arms.

When he pushed the door to the main floor open, he was surprised to see two red-helmeted firemen passing by, one of them carrying an axe. He followed them to the lounge, and placed Irene on an overstuffed chair near a tall artificial green plant.

It soon became apparent that though all the power had come back on, the elevator doors, just ahead, were still shut tight and refused to budge open. Jerry saw the two firemen talking with a fellow who might be a maintenance man. He looked around the lobby and couldn't catch a glimpse of Lylah anywhere, not even down by the glass doors to the emergency room.

Well, maybe she had found Dr. Barrow and they were together, still talking to Gary's room mate. Jerry thought he recognized the younger fireman as a boy he had taught about five years ago at Rosemont High. Nurse Debbie made eye contact with him and gave him a little friendly wave.

"That's my boyfriend, Steve," she said to Jerry. "I'm going over to see what's going on."

Looking down, he saw his daughter was already sleeping. It made him realize how tired he was, too, so he sat down with her, putting her comfortably on his lap. Shutting his eyes, he realized how quiet the hospital was - the awful storm had finally passed.

Less than a minute later, Fire chief Larry's loud voice woke Jerry from his brief sleep.

"If there's anybody inside, step away from the doors! We're coming in!"

Steve struck a heavy blow with his axe, and the loud slam and crunch of metal on metal reverberated through the lobby. He twisted the blade from side to side, and then the two men, using their gloved hands, managed to pull the doors open. For some reason, Jerry found himself drawn toward the activity near the newly opened doors. A cluster of others, staff mostly, as well as patients' relatives, no doubt, also moved forward to get a look.

Then he saw a few women up front turn their faces away, aghast at whatever they'd seen. A man yelled, "Oh, fuck!" as both firemen moved into the interior of the elevator.

Jerry had the odd sensation of thinking the walls around this large lobby space were moving closer, closing him in and creating a rush of air that propelled him around the other scattered observers, toward the firemen. And as he moved forward, he remembered words that someone - Dr. Barrow? - had said to him thirteen years ago.

"Jerry, your wife was found dead on the elevator floor when the doors opened in the lobby."

Here he was, thirteen years older but no wiser, standing near the very same spot to see . . .

A large crack in the elevator's ceiling allowed one long stockinged leg and an arm, partially covered by a length of blue satin cloth, to hang suspended above the floor. A torn section of a silk slip adhered to the thigh, and a long red wire of blood ran down the slightly swinging arm to drip red onto the hard gray rubbery surface below.

The younger fireman reached up as if to help pull her down, but the chief pulled him back.

"It's no good, kid - she's gone. If we start tugging, we'll just cut her up even worse. She must have fallen from one of the top floors. We'll have to take that ceiling down. Let's rope this whole area off - "

But Jerry had moved in close and seen a glint of something on the floor, just to one side of the scarlet puddle.

"Chief -" he said hoarsely, "can you see what that is?"

And he pointed down at the small rectangular object.

The chief picked it up and read the name on its surface.

"Nurse Lylah Peake," he said, "Know her?"

Jerry recoiled, began walking backwards, shaking his head back and forth repeatedly, causing the chief to interpret that as a "no." So both firemen were shocked to see him collapse on the lobby floor, giving the back of his head a good crack on the edge of a low glass table.
******

He woke up a half hour later on a gurney in a hallway just outside the emergency room.

When he moved to get up, a woman's hand shoved his shoulder back on the thin mattress.

"We just took an x-ray. You knocked yourself out on the edge of a table. Nurse Nelson will be back in a minute - she's with the police. We're all a mess about Penny, poor thing. Poor thing. Remain lying flat, please."

73

He strained his head and read her name tag, "Dearborn." Her pale face was nearly covered with freckles, and behind her dark black framed glasses, he could see she'd been crying.

"My son and daughter, where are they?"

"I'm right here, Dad."

He twisted his sore head the other way, and there was Gary.

"They just took Irene back up to her room. Doc Barrow says we can all go home in a little while. There's a detective wants to talk with you. The joint is crawling with cops now."

The young man looked around nervously, at a loss for a way to continue.

"I don't know what to say, Dad. . . I'm sorry about Lylah, you know. What an awful way . . ."

Shocked to see his son's lips trembling with emotion, Jerry was equally disturbed by the absence of any such feeling himself. Gary went on.

"I wish I hadn't always given her such a hard time, see. She tried her best with us, I guess -"

Jerry reached out and punched the boy's arm.

"Hey - hey - none of that, hear me! You and I need to have a talk, okay?"

He grabbed the sleeve of Gary's shirt, pulling him closer.

"Not here, not now, but later - at home. There are things you don't know, things she just told me tonight."

"Okay, okay . . ."

"Look at you - where did you get those crazy clothes?"

Gary smiled broadly.

"One of the nurses, a male nurse, loaned me his stuff - got them from his locker. I said I'd return them later."

"You look like one of those hippies or something, in those pants."

"Stripes, Dad, they're only stripes. And the shirt - it's paisley."

Jerry, grateful for the laugh he was having , saw the nurse had gone, and struggled to sit up.

Barrow, looking haggard and preoccupied, suddenly, almost as if by magic, was at his side.

"You feeling better? How's the head?"

"Sore."

The doctor's fingers on the back of his head felt instantly relaxing, soothing and familiar in a way that made him think of Vera - not Lylah.

"An old acquaintance of mine, a cop named Silkworth, wants to have a few words with you. I think he's an okay guy, but he's what we used to call a slippery customer. Made a lot of enemies in this town. I'm needed down the hall now, Jerry. See you in a few minutes."

Over Barrow's shoulder, he'd already caught sight of a very tall, imposing figure, obviously someone of authority, coming toward him. He looked sixty-ish and was wearing a belted raincoat and brown fedora.

"Would you be Mr. Todd?" he asked, looking right at Jerry.

"Yeah, Jerry."

"I'm Detective Silkworth - sorry about your wife, sir."

Gary's head came into view from around a corner to say he was going back up to Irene's room to try and move things along.

The detective noticed a folding chair next to the gurney and sat down. Jerry figured he was self-conscious about his height and might not want to appear threatening. Sitting on the edge of the mattress, however, Jerry saw little of the man's face, but only heard his voice from underneath the wide brim of his hat.

"So, Mr. Todd . . . I know you have a lot to deal with, but I really need to ask you a few questions."

"Of course."

"I wasn't called in on this for your wife's death, because that was clearly an accident, due to a power failure - but you know what's funny? My wife- she reads

75

lots of these Agatha Christie books, who-done-its? - you know?"

Still the face was hidden. Jerry felt like sitting on the floor just to tick the guy off. Silkworth had more to say.

"I have a feeling a really good writer would find a way to tie the power failure to the murder in some way. Kind of like the old chestnut where the lights go out, and when they come back on, there's this dead body, and the detective has to solve the crime."

Jerry couldn't believe what he was hearing.

"Was there a question in there somewhere?"

Silkworth used his thumb to lift his hat a few inches up his brow.

"Mr. Todd," he said, "I don't mean to make light of what's happened here tonight, but - I tell you, it's one for the record books. The whole weather thing is what's driving me bonkers cause, of course, it can't have anything to do with the murder in the dispensary - there's the title Christie would have used, don't you think? Murder in the Dispensary.

"Who did it? . . . Well, I'm afraid I do believe - for whatever reason - I do believe it was your poor wife, Mr. Todd. The young nurse, it seems, let her into the room, where they seem to keep an array of supplies. You should see what a mess that room is. It's more like a catch-all storage room for everything under the sun - so that's our crime scene. Your wife told this young Miss Nelson she'd been assigned to this hospital for the night. Minutes later, as I see it, Nurse Penny went in and confronted her, and was stabbed to death by this strange, caped nurse who DID, once upon a time, work here - years ago, is that a fact?"

"Yes, detective, that's a fact."

My question for you is, do you have any idea why your wife was wearing her nurse's uniform and cape here tonight?"

———

"No, I don't, but I can tell you my wife received a great shock this afternoon. We met with Dr. Barrow about - "

"Yes, he told me about that awful diagnosis- do you know John and I were classmates at Rosemont High years ago? And you currently teach there, don't you?"

"I do. When did you graduate?"

"Oh, in the dark ages - before Elvis - hell, before Sinatra. . . so, she sort of got a death sentence, a brain tumor, was it?"

"Yes. I think Lylah was delusional tonight."

"You base that on what?"

"Things she said to me, crazy things. Let's just say - and I want you to know it's not easy for me to say this - that I support your conclusion about what she did tonight. Do you think we might meet again a few days from now - there are things I want to tell you, but I've got relatives to call, two kids to deal with, an undertaker to talk to . . . You see, frankly I need time to sort all this shit out."

"That makes two of us, young fella."

The weary detective stood up, all six foot five inches of him, and placed a reassuring hand on Jerry's shoulder. But there was one more thing he needed to say.

"John Barrow says he was with you down here when the lights went out, and it was then you ran upstairs to check on your daughter. Nurse Debbie- she's quite a honey, by the way- met you upstairs when you came out of the stairwell, and she says she accompanied you around the corner to the elevator where you found your little girl. The murder must have taken place minutes before the power failure - in the dispensary, when your unfortunate wife was in, to quote you, a delusional state. Not long after the murder, for some reason, she fell to her death down the elevator shaft. You know what I say to that,Mr. Todd?"

Jerry shook his head, then added, "Unless it means I have an alibi."

"I say it means 'case closed.' At least until I see you . . . In a week or so?"

"Absolutely - you have your office in the municipal building on Merritt Street?"

Silkworth smiled.

"I have a desk there. Same one since 1958. Oh, yes, the second question, a quick one. Barrow noticed a bandage on your wife's hand - her palm? Do you know how she injured it?"

"No. I noticed it when she came back from the house with some clothes to spend the night here. She brushed it off, didn't seem to want to talk about it. Maybe she'd been handling a knife in the kitchen?"

Silkworth shook his head.

"Doc says it's a burn, a deep, nasty one. Well, Mr. Todd, I'll let you get on with your family business. Again, my condolences."

The detective reached in his coat pocket and handed Jerry his card.

"My home number's written on the back. Call any time, if you think of anything you want to talk about- okay?"

He lowered the wide brim of his hat, turned and pushed his way through a glass door back to the lobby.

Chapter 14: Home - 11:15 PM

A little less than an hour later, they were homeward bound in their car. Lylah's scent, her lilac perfume, rode with them. Jerry gave her a bottle of it every Christmas, and like other traditions, it would end tonight. Gary sat in the back seat, Irene next to her father in the front.

"I had a funny dream in the hospital tonight," she said, as they headed out of the parking lot.

"And I suppose," said Gary, "we're gonna have to hear about it, huh?"

"Don't let your dreams bother you, honey. The nurses gave you some medicine that might have caused weird dreams, that's all."

But she told her father the dream was caused by the pictures he had shown her the other day. He'd brought out an old photo album of a vacation he and some friends had taken out West, one summer when he was in college.

"What pictures caused the nightmare?"

"It wasn't exactly a nightmare- I mean at first it was, but then it wasn't."

"Good," said Gary, "you know, there's a theory that if you don't talk about your dreams, you'll be better able to forget them - Dad, that cop's car just passed us."

Jerry looked ahead and caught a glimpse of the wide brimmed hat through the car's rear window. Silkworth's unmarked car sped ahead and exited on the Main St. ramp.

"You know," said Gary, "he's kind of a nice guy - for a cop."

"Yeah," agreed Jerry, "and you're a nice guy - for a hippie. Now, let Irene finish her story."

"Yeah Ga-ree!" she shouted teasingly, then continued.

"It was those pictures of the caves with all the bats. And I was hanging upside down, stuck to one of the high walls of a cave. I was one of them, sort of. Then the bats all flew away and left me there."

"Carlsbad," interrupted Gary, behind her.

Irene twisted her head around menacingly.

"Oh yeah," she said, "what did Carl do that was so bad, Ga-ree?"

Jerry laughed.

"Hah, she got you there! Good one, kid!"

"Mom told you not to call me that, remember."

A sudden silence descended over the car. Then, as they made the turn by the Dairy Queen, Irene was the first to break it.

"It's okay," she said, "I know she's not coming back. She's dead. A nurse told me she fell down the steps or something."

Jerry cleared his throat and asked her how the dream ended.

"I wanted to fly away, too, but couldn't. Then I looked down and I saw you way down there, Dad. I crawled down slowly toward you, and you reached up and pulled me down."

She hunkered down and slid closer to him.

"I don't know," she said, "what I was doing up there in the cave."

Jerry whispered to her that he knew exactly what she was doing there. She looked up at him.

"What?"

He squeezed her earlobe with his free hand, saying softly, "Just hanging around, honey."

"Here I am," said Gary, "back here, the only sensible one in the family."

Cheshire Street, theirs, was just up ahead.

———

***** ***** *****
.   .
11:30 PM.

Gary told his father he'd help Irene get ready for bed. Even though she said she was eleven and old enough to get ready herself, Jerry could tell she would allow him to help her out - just a little.

The first thing Jerry noticed when he walked into the master bedroom was a faint odor of burning. Turning the lights on, he saw the patch of rough, charred carpet on the far side of the bed, way too large to have been caused by a lit cigarette. He opened the window and felt a cool draft he knew would quickly clear the odor. Then he looked on the bed, where he saw the familiar metal box, as well as its contents, next to it on the spread: a few folded papers he recalled reading once or twice over the years, and the stone itself, which he also remembered seeing several times over the years - Egg-shaped with those peculiar carved lines going from the narrow top of the oval to the wider bottom. And there were those two triangular protrusions at the top that resembled, he'd always thought, ears - looking exactly as it had always looked.

But hadn't Lylah told him the stone had disappeared or shrunk tonight? He looked again at the carpet and remembered what Silkworth had said about Lylah's burned hand.

The easiest explanation, of course, was that most of what she described was the product of a confused, even deranged, mind. Wandering around the hospital wearing her old uniform, stabbing Nurse Penny . . . Jerry wanted, above all, to start to get things back to normal. So, after putting the stone and the papers back in the box, he carried it downstairs.

***** ***** *****
.   .

MIDNIGHT

After making the family phone calls to his mother in Scranton and his brother-law in Baltimore, as well as a few others, he went into the kitchen and saw Gary and Irene had already raided the fridge for snacks and gone upstairs for the night. Hearing nothing but complete silence, he went back to the desk in the den, grabbed the metal box and carried it outside to the car. Noting that the air had turned oddly warm and humid after the storm, especially for November, he opened the trunk, placed the box inside next to the spare and went back inside.
Too exhausted to even attempt the stairs, he gave in to the temptation of the living room couch and fell instantly asleep.

Nearly an hour later he opened his eyes, and they were staring at the open front door. Checking his watch, he saw it was 12:45 a.m. Had someone gone out? - come in? He got up, went to the doorway and gazed across the front yard and driveway.

Standing next to the car, Gary stood, wearing only white pajama pants and staring over the car's roof at the shadowy neighborhood. His bare back in the moonlight looked strangely dark, muscled in a way Jerry had never before noticed. He didn't move as his father approached.

Jerry hesitated before placing his hand on his son's shoulder.

"Gary, what are you doing?"

He turned his head slowly, a severe, almost threatening light in his eyes.

"Standing guard."

"Standing guard! Over what?"

Instead of responding, Gary simply looked down at the car and placed his hand on the trunk.

Jerry looked down and saw he was wearing sandals, held in place with two simple leather ropes.

"You're practically in your bare feet . . . I didn't know you had sandals."

The young man was rubbing his fingers through his hair, as though coming to his senses. His next words were nearly mumbled.

"Mom bought them for me in September before I went back to college."

Jerry drew back his head as though slapped.

"Mom?"

His son had never used the word naturally before.

"Look, Dad, I don't know what's going on. Let's get inside. What's wrong with me? I don't remember leaving the house."

"We've all been under a lot of stress today. Come on . . . " Jerry's fingers felt for the stiff surface of Silkworth's card in his shirt pocket, then followed his son into the house.

***** ***** *****

Middle of the Night

Silkworth had barely recognized Jerry's shaky voice when he got the call twenty minutes ago. The new widower, obviously rattled by recent events, wanted to give him some information, as well as "an object I need to get out of my house." Intrigued, the detective headed to his car for the fifteen minute drive to Cheshire Avenue. Jerry said he'd have the front porch light on, and when he made the turn from Main Street, he immediately saw the solitary glow from number thirty-two Cheshire, at the far end of the second block. Pulling along side Jerry's Chevy in the driveway, he got out and made his way up to the front door, already open behind the screen door.

Inside, Jerry greeted the detective and asked him to come into the kitchen, where Gary was pouring coffee, with a trembling hand, into three cups. Jerry insisted on telling both of them, at the same time, what Lylah had confessed to just hours ago in the hospital. As Jerry expected, his son was visibly shaken by hearing his mother had not died of a heart attack, years ago, but had been cruelly poisoned by the woman who, within a year, became his step mother.

"You have to believe me," Jerry said to Gary, "I had no idea about any of this until tonight. I could never have lived with this woman if I even had a suspicion of this."

Then, as Silkworth listened more intently than he had ever listened to anyone, Jerry recounted the strange emotional problems Irene had been exhibiting these past months - that had reached their climax today in Doc Barrow's office, then later tonight in the elevator shaft. These incidents, along with Lylah's delusions, all seemed due to the presence in the house of this odd Egyptian stone in this metal box, which now rested on the kitchen table in a paper bag next to a dish of cookies - right under Silkworth's face. Jerry quickly summarized the key elements regarding how the artifact came into Lylah's family.

"Don't open the box now, please? And don't keep it in your house. Keep it in your office- or desk. We can talk more about this in a week or so, after the funeral. I just need it out of here tonight . . . It's been destroying my family."

Gary was nodding his head, seemingly speechless.

Jerry reminded the detective that there were papers in the box containing more information he might want to read tomorrow.

He reached across the table, sliding the bag closer to Silkworth - doubtlessly signaling his speech was over.

The detective started to get up, but then realized one thing remained he needed to clarify.

"Tell me, Jerry, am I to understand that Lylah died in the very same hospital elevator where your first wife died - as a result of being poisoned by Lylah - thirteen years ago?"

Long seconds of silence passed at the table. Finally, Jerry nodded his head, and the detective slapped the table surface with the palm of his hand.

"Well!" he exclaimed.

"Well what?" asked Gary.

"Perfect justice, I'd say. One thing I want to caution you about, Mr. Todd, is not to leak any ideas out about your suspicions regarding your first wife being murdered - especially since her murderer is no longer alive. It would all just make the police department back then seem . . . deficient in some way. The coroner at the time is, even to this day, a very respectable man, by the way. Yes, such a re-examination of that old case would paint many of us in a bad light, I'm afraid. Don't you think?"

"I suppose," said Jerry, "and yet , as unpleasant as it might be - perhaps we owe it to Vera's memory to get the truth -"

"Believe me, Jerry, the last thing you and your boy want to do is to go to a newspaper reporter with any of these murder ideas. . . best to let sleeping dogs lie, right?"

Jerry's eyes met his son's for a few somber seconds.

"I just don't know," said Jerry. "Vera's parents are still living, you see, and to this day they hold themselves responsible for causing her death. They feel they neglected to insist she continue seeing a doctor about her heart . . ."

Jerry was getting the idea that Silkworth had been down this road many times before. Certainly this couldn't be the first time he was overstepping his authority in sweeping the truth under the rug. Barrow, no doubt was right - a slippery customer indeed.

"Perfect justice, gentlemen," continued the detective, " - one doesn't see it very often. Sometimes perhaps other forces, besides law and order, can intervene to produce it . . . call it justice of a rougher kind. Well, good luck, you folks. I'll take my souvenir and see you, Mr. Todd - in about a week."

He grabbed the brown paper bag from the table, turned and walked outside.

The eastern sky was already brightening with a hint of dawn as he got behind the wheel, placing the bag on the seat next to him. He smiled at the thought of telling his wife about all this in a few hours, when she'd ask-as always - "So, what's new, Sherlock?"

Feeling a bit warm, he rolled his window down, at once hearing a nearby stereo blaring one of his favorite songs from some years back. One of the Todds' early-bird neighbors waking more than a few sleepers with - was it Joni Mitchell's version - of - ?

He backed out of the driveway, heading slowly down Cheshire.

From the front bedroom window of the Todd house, Irene watched his vehicle glide down the street. Shocked, she saw it flash into a ball of fire, the force of the explosion jolting her back a few feet toward her bed. Downstairs, she heard a commotion, and, back at her window again, she watched as her brother and father raced out onto the lawn below. From the fireball of the wreckage in the middle of the road, the driver emerged, stumbling and waving fiery arms against the darkness. Finally, she saw the man collapse on the pavement. Their own property, although a block away from the inferno, was alive with the orange glow. She opened the window and leaned out to get a better look.

"See the pyramids along the Nile,
Watch the sunrise on a tropic isle,
Just remember, darling, all the while -
You belong to me."

THE END

◻

———

86

DASH

PROLOGUE

This is a most extraordinary story, if you don't mind me saying so up front. It takes place in a small city in the foothills of the Pocono Mountains in northeastern Pennsylvania in the 1960's. So far in the past it would seem appropriate to begin with the words "Once upon a time . . ."

Those old enough to recall those years often label them as difficult times. I think it was the British who, ages ago, referred to their own troubled era, with some irony, as years when "god's in his heaven and all is right with the world."

Only a lunatic would say such a thing about the 1960's, or today, for that matter, unless he had a truckload of irony. Still, as bad as things were on both the national and global scene, we lacked, then, the twenty-four-hour news channels and internet that so magnify and intensify our current chaos. It was possible in those days, believe it or not - with just a little effort -to remove one's self for long periods of time from unpleasant reports in the daily papers, and turn a blind eye and a deaf ear to the radio and TV news broadcasts that were doing their best to break through the strained tranquility of our town - let's call it Rosemont, shall we? Rosemont, Pennsylvania, 1968, where many of its citizens were trying to block out the assassinations, the Manson murders, the endless stream of dead soldiers coming home from Vietnam; a handful of others, however, even in our city, were indeed making their own dark contributions to the fabric of a society that was fraying around the edges, at the very least.

We couldn't help but think, in those bygone days, that almost anything might be possible . . . even in Rosemont.

ONE

Early afternoon at the Grady Free Library, two blocks from Public Square, on an unusually cool summer afternoon. It must have been about a week after the fourth of July, and I was at my usual station. Exactly where I was supposed to be when the head librarian and my supervisor, Mrs. Drest, was on her lunch break. Standing behind the main counter, I was attempting to look both helpful and authoritative. Not easy to do, you try it sometime.

I had turned my back to place a few recently returned books on a cart for future shelving, when I heard, for the first time, Bea Wood's voice, low but oddly resonant.

"Can you help me find a path to destruction?"

Catching at once the clever joke she was making, I did not immediately turn to face her. Only a few weeks ago I'd ended what had become, at least for me, a disastrous dating experience, and didn't think I was ready to begin another. So, I counted slowly to ten before facing her.

Her face, almost but not quite perfectly round, was topped by a row of Beatlesque bangs just above her eyes, the lashes of which were heavily embroidered with whatever gook it is that some girls use to decorate them. Likewise, her lips were burdened with a slash of red that now parted into the faintest grin when she saw she had my attention. Her two clenched fists supported each side of her chin, somewhat coquettishly, her elbows resting on my counter. An odd notion occurred to me that she just might be fully prepared to remain fixed in that pose all afternoon.

No one else had heard her- Mrs. Drest wasn't due back for another fifteen minutes- but I raised my finger for her to be patient for a second, while I feigned interest in some index cards that were luckily within my reach. Head lowered, this time I only counted to five before looking up to walk the three steps or so toward her.

"You mean, of course, the new Edna Blither novel?"

"Well now, what do YOU think? I thought it amusing to use the title that way, but perhaps you don't have a sense of humor?"

Even though I'd recently made a solemn promise never to show my cards too soon to a girl again, I did sense her eagerness for a friendly smile. I gave her instead a business type scowl and directed her to the "new arrivals" shelves just to her right.

"The book came in a few days ago, miss. It should be there - alphabetical order according to the author's last name."

As she walked away to search, I saw that the hemline of her yellow dress barely reached the back of her knees. Not quite as short of fabric as these miniskirts that were becoming so popular, but definitely shocking enough for Rosemont. Still, its shortness added some length to her legs, whereas a longer dress would only cause her to appear almost dwarfish. She might have been five foot two, but certainly not much more. I could also see that her hair in the back was done up in a complicated bun. An unexpected twist in a novel or story might be welcome, but in a hairdo it's merely a complication that should just be, well, cut.

The main reading room had more than a few empty tables, not unusual for a weekday afternoon in summer, and certainly none of the students there were even remotely interested in my hesitant, perhaps even pathetic attempt to assist her as she traced a finger along the top shelf, searching for this current best seller.

"Oh dear, oh dear. . ." I intoned mournfully, now suddenly standing just to the left of the bun itself. "It seems someone has beaten you to it."

"Oh, gosh - and I was so looking forward to having it for the weekend!"

"I'll check when it's due back."

She followed me to the counter and on the way gave out a girlish squeal of amazement. I knew instantly it had been designed to stop me in my tracks and turn to see what had caught her attention. But sticking to my purpose, I rifled through the cards of borrowed books until I located the information she needed.

"It's due back on the fifth of August, miss."

She just HAD to tell me why she had almost cried out - she'd seen a ray of sunlight streaming through one of the stained-glass windows in the east wall. To her it made the entire place seem almost church-like. I replied that Mrs. Drest would certainly agree and often remarked herself that the library was indeed a holy place.

"Why, you sound like you're devoted to your boss."

"She's sort of my supervisor, but we get along. She's been here more than fifteen years."

"You don't mind taking orders from a woman?"

"Not if she's sensible and level-headed."

"And you don't have another copy?"

"Of what?"

"My book, silly!"

"We would have seen it on the shelf if we had." She knew she'd distracted me, and I quickly felt I was losing points in my struggle to remain aloof.

Then she startled me by remarking that she thought she knew me from the hospital.

"Why? Do I look ill?"

"No," she blushed, and I saw it did nothing for her complexion. "I thought you might have come there to visit someone recently. I'm on the nursing staff there."

"You must be confusing me with someone else, I'm afraid. It's been years since I've been in a hospital."

Her lips curved downward in a disappointed frown.

"Really? I could have sworn. . ."

She abruptly extended a hand with surprisingly long red-nailed fingers under my face.

"Well, I'm Bea - Bea Wood."

"There's my name," I said, gesturing to the little engraved plastic sign just under her very eyes on the counter. Her handshake was oddly firm for a girl, while mine, I'm afraid, was just as oddly, weak.

"Oh! How professional, Mr. Shifter! Do you have a first name?"

"Doesn't everyone?" And I was perfectly straight-faced.

Near us, the front doors opened and Mrs. Drest, back from a quick lunch, seemed at once curious as to what might be the nature of my interaction with this creature from the outside world. The head librarian might have been just old enough to be my mother but still carried a shapely figure underneath clothes that were, well, generally distinctive but had an almost theatrical flare. Today her gray skirt was topped off by a raised piece of yellow quilted material that wrapped around her tummy like a sash. And a large green and yellow flowered pin glared from her white blouse.

"Mrs. Drest, this young lady was just wondering -"

"But we shouldn't bother your supervisor with -"

Mrs. Drest silenced both of us by putting her frequently raised finger to her thin lips, removing her red sweater and coming over to stand at my side, exuding her familiar lilac perfume scent.

"She wants to know if we have a second copy of "Path to Destruction.""

A terrified expression enlivened the woman's blank face.

"Oh, for silly's sake!"

I never did find out the source of that distinctive exclamation of hers. Sometimes I hear it in my dreams - to this day, but I don't want to get ahead of myself.

In a flutter of phrases, she explained that she herself had been perusing that very book minutes before going for lunch. Of course, she never would have dreamt of taking it from the premises to read over lunch - there were specific rules forbidding -

By now she was talking to herself behind the glass enclosure of her private office on the other side of the counter.

"It did hold my interest for a chapter or so. I certainly can see why it's created such a stir. Oh, here it is -"

Out of her lair, quick as a bat with the very book in hand, she zeroed in with precision on the pretty young fiction lover. Clearly, I no longer existed for my older colleague, so I tried my best to fade and blend into the children's section near the main door. I heard squeals of pleasure from both of them as they finalized the transaction regarding the book.

Miss Wood did cast a rapid glance my way and saw me raise my own finger to my lips in mockery of Mrs. Drest, or Mrs. UNdrest, as the janitor often referred to her.

I headed for the nearby water cooler, where I waited, sipping slowly from a paper cup.

"You should have an exciting weekend now," I said when she arrived at my side.

"My friends are going to the shore, so I've nothing else to do but read, you see." We were both whispering now in deference to library protocol.

"If you've nothing better to do - "I began, feeling my recent vow of caution dissolving like an icicle in my brain - "we could go to a movie Saturday night."

TWO

The movie on Saturday night was Bonnie and Clyde, which we both wanted to see because it had been condemned by the Legion of Decency. So afterwards at a restaurant on Public Square, just around the corner from the theater, we sat in a booth and talked about how out of step the Catholic church was with the real world. Bea frankly admitted she believed there was no such thing as god. I couldn't help laughing aloud.

"What's so funny? Plenty of intelligent people are atheists."

"No, Bea, it isn't that - I just think it's funny that after seeing that particular movie, we're talking about religion."

She wanted to know if I'd rather talk about gangsters, and feeling she was getting seriously annoyed, I changed the subject by talking about my father.

"His father, my grandfather, was an Episcopalian minister, and sad to say, I fear they'd both agree with the legion about this movie - especially the violence."

"Well," she said, "perhaps it's something children shouldn't see, but as a nurse I have no problem with seeing bloodshed - really it is a part of life, isn't it?"

Then a strange question, I thought.

"Are you close to your parents, Jeremy?"

"Yes, as a matter of fact, I tried to get a position in the Allentown area - just to stay close to home. But that didn't work out."

Behind me the restaurant's front door opened, and a blast of cool air hit my neck. She looked up and over my shoulder. I at once heard the familiar voice of my best friend since childhood - Dash.

We had both grown up on the same street in a suburb of Allentown, attended the same schools there, including college. And finally, it was he who suggested I send my resume out to Rosemont's Grady Library. He had come to this very town the year before to become assistant manager in his distant cousin's auto body center. I'd already begun to badly miss his company and was very happy when I was eventually hired there.

"Well, Dot, old man, I thought I recognized the back of your handsome head!"

Bea laughed, I felt, a little too hard, while I turned and made room on the bench next to me for him to sit. He did, quickly extending his hand to her.

"I'm Paul," he said, "but your date and I have annoying nicknames for each other. I call him Dot and he calls me Dash."

She made a grimace.

"I'm trying to decide," she said, "whether that's oh so charming or oh so strange."

I piped up with the comment that it was I, as Dot, who got the worst of the arrangement.

"It's more of a girlish name, isn't it?" I asked. "Sort of a shortened form of Dorothy - where he gets the better name of Dash."

I slapped my hand warmly on his shoulder and looked at Bea.

"Go ahead," I prompted her, "you've got to ask . . ."

"Okay," she said, looking directly into Dash's cool green eyes, "how did you two get those crazy nicknames?"

Leo, our waiter and one of the owner's sons, put our cheeseburgers on the table and asked Dash if he wanted anything.

"Just coffee, Leo," he said and turned to me.

"Shall I do the honors?" he asked.

"Go ahead," I said, then looking at Bea, added, "he IS the better story-teller."

So, while she and I munched on our cheeseburgers, he waited for his coffee, lit a cigarette and began the tale of the nicknames: how in seventh grade we had become obsessed with Morse code, read everything we could get our hands on about the inventor and his experiments, and one whole summer would phone each other late at night to make goofy noises across the tiny holes on the phone's voice receiver to mimic the sounds of dots and dashes.

Finally, seeing how captivated she was by his narration, I interrupted.

"It was his father who came up with the nicknames for us, Bea."

Her mouth moved oddly, almost sideways, as she chewed, in a manner I found distracting and slightly repulsive. But, sitting just to my right, Dash stared at her, seemingly fascinated.

She asked him what he did for a living, and he talked for a while about his work as supervisor at the new auto body repair shop out on Market Street. Then she inquired about his parents, her lips quivering with seemingly genuine sorrow as he recounted - briefly, thank god- the events concerning their sudden deaths just last year in a car accident on the turnpike, adding also that as an only child how hard it was for him to accept. He pointed his thumb in my direction and told her he wouldn't have been able to get through those rough days without me.

She did look at me then, just a quick glance, though.

"Yeah," I said, "we go back a long time. Do you have any close friends, Bea?"

"Oh, a few. Tell me, Paul, where do you live?"

Very interested she was in the details about his two-bedroom apartment on Chestnut street. He had just moved into it a few months ago after selling the family home in Allentown. She'd just love to see it because she herself might one of these days be looking for her own place and was anxious to get an idea of what "apartment living" might be like. She had spoken to me earlier about how difficult it had become for her to share even her own large house with just one other person, her father. Though Bea claimed to have great affection for her dad, she felt he often treated her like one of his biology students at the college.

Ever sociable, Dash suggested we come over to his place now. He had a six pack in the fridge, and if we hurried we could watch his favorite TV show, "Thriller.

"Boris Karloff cracks me up," he said, flashing his sexiest grin right at her.

"Beer and Karloff, Bea - how can we resist?" I was trying my best to appear eager for the merriment to continue.

We made our way toward Leo at the cash register near the door. I was not yet completely sure she had totally lost interest in me. That came about five minutes later when I found myself alone in Dash's back seat, while she sat up front next to him as he drove us to his place.

I contemplated again the strange twist of hair on the back of her head. In the passing glares of the streetlights it almost seemed to be uncoiling.

THREE

I saw her two or three times after that, but it became clear that whatever sparks were supposed to ignite were nowhere on the scene for us. So, one afternoon when I had promised to phone her, I didn't. I kept expecting her either to call me or stop by the library in person to see what was going on, but she never did. Then one afternoon Dash DID drop by with news that she had phoned him the night before to see how he was doing, said she gave him the impression we were no longer an item. He felt obligated, however, to check with me before asking her out himself.

"She's all yours, buddy."

"No hard feelings?"

"None."

It was also around that time that the book she'd checked out turned up in the returns bin when Mrs. Drest was at her post.

"That girl you were so taken with returned that book."

"I only saw her a couple of times."

She nodded her head, conveying more than slight approval, then told me something rather startling.

"I did some checking on her. She's a nurse at St. Luke's Hospital, still lives at home with her father, who was asked to leave his position as science professor at our university a couple of years ago."

"Asked to leave? Under what circumstances - do you know?"

"No, it all seems very mysterious. My source at the university generally knows everything, but it seems a very tight lid was put on the whole business for some reason."

She was looking over my shoulder at a few young men who had just opened the main door and added that I was no doubt "well rid of her."

Bea had told me a little about her father, seemed rather fond of him, referring to him jokingly as the original mad scientist. She'd given the impression he was currently a professor of some sort and had never said a word to me about his dismissal from any position. I couldn't help wondering why Mrs. Drest had taken such an interest in Bea, but just when I was about to press her on this point, she was distracted by the loud talking of those students and rushed off to quiet them.

It was about a month later, as the summer was winding down, that Mrs. Drest, this time wearing a rather tight straight light blue dress with what looked like brown leather shoulder straps and matching rustic leather belt, approached me in the deserted History aisle.

"Perhaps I am just a busybody, but I can't help feeling a bit protective of you. I hope you won't think ill of me for again telling you something I heard about that Wood creature?"

"Of course not. What have you heard?"

"She and a boyfriend were in a whale of a fight at the Carousel the other night. The manager had to call the cops. My brother told me they had to "sleep it off" in the jail overnight. Her father ended up paying for the damage at the bar, settled things with the cops and then drove the love birds home - for silly's sake, can you imagine!"

Then, with what seemed genuine worry: "You are so lucky to have nipped that in the bud, Jeremy."

"Thanks, Mrs. Drest. It's good to know there's someone looking out for me," I said.

I didn't tell her, then, how close a friend Bea's new fella was to me.

Mrs. Drest raised her hand and brushed some hairs back from my brow.

"With your high forehead, you know, you're going to be bald before you're forty - poor fellow."

She turned and walked back to the main reading room.

Believing I had witnessed nothing more than her maternal instinct, I shrugged the awkward moment off.

*****

Only a few days later Dash was waiting for me on the sidewalk when my shift was over, so it must have been around 4:30. It was mid-September and colder air had been rolling down from the mountains the past few days, sending swirls of newly fallen leaves now all along Franklin Street. Dash had his hands in the pockets of his dark blue pea coat, its collar turned up around his neck. We hardly ever met like this, and, judging by his serious expression, I could tell something was wrong. He suggested the counter at Drake's for coffee, adding he needed to discuss something with me.

"Oh, you two!" the waitress shouted our way when we came in. Emma, overbearing but slyly amusing, acted like she owned the place, even though Big Ed, the actual owner, had hired her only last winter. She had, however, quickly endeared herself to many of the regular male customers with her easy, familiar ways. On more than one occasion she'd told Dash and me that she'd love to take us home with her but that she'd be accused of robbing the cradle. I gave her a big hello, but after bringing us our coffee, she seemed to sense Dash's solemn mood and retreated back to the kitchen.

"So, what's going on, kid?" I asked.

"Uncle Sam, that's what's going on."

He slid an official looking envelope my way with the local draft board's address visible in the left corner.

"Fucking LBJ," he muttered, then added, "can't you lend me your heart, Dot?"

This was a reference to my heart murmur, discovered about four months earlier when I'd received my own summons and gone for my physical. There was a bit more to it than that, of course.

"I've got to report for my physical next week. I told Bea last night."

"How did she take it?"

"Frankly, I was surprised how upset she was. She wants us to make a run for Canada."

I told him I didn't think she'd ever abandon her father, and he said she'd probably calm down and get used to the idea in a few days.

"Couples," he said, "have to adjust to long separations in wartime. That's what her old man told us."

"Is that what you two are now - a couple?"

"Well, yeah, sort of - I guess. I suggested she could move into my place while I'm away and keep the home fires burning so to speak until I get back. Told her it would give her a little independence at least. But she doesn't like to hear any criticism about dear old Dad. There's something a bit creepy about him, though I can't put my finger on it. He's been complaining of weird headaches lately, so she says. Later, at my place, that's when she got hysterical and started babbling about Canada. Jesus, I told her, it's ME who's being drafted, not you. Then, honest to god, Dot, she came at me and was covering me with kisses and practically ripping my clothes off, saying she can't bear the idea of us separating. Got really aggressive in the love-making department, let me tell you, buddy."

I'd never heard him talk about or describe a girl in this way and saw his face turn red with embarrassment. He covered it well, though, by adding that maybe the military discipline would be just what he might need to get him "out of her clutches."

His words, not mine.

Then he said that tomorrow was her birthday and wanted me to come with him to help him pick out a gift - said he knew just what she wanted: a puppy. So, we left a generous tip on the counter for Emma and headed to Pat's Pet Store on Main Street. He and Bea had been there a few days ago, and she had fallen in love with a tiny German Shepherd that was still on display in the storefront window when we got there. It was cute enough for sure, yapping away at us from behind the glass - though not the sort of dog you'd think a girl would choose. Mostly gray and black splotches of sleek short hairs and a narrow-pointed snout, it seemed to me like it would quickly turn into a wolf.

FOUR

Dear Dot,

      As my best friend, I know I can trust you not to tell anyone about this letter. The only other person who knows about our plans to head north is Bea's father, who's following us as far as Niagara Falls in his car. He's been really great, has given us a lot of cash and actually seems to like me for some reason. I told him about you, gave him your address, so he promises to contact you every now and then with news about Bea and me - there's a funny title for this new chapter of my life: Bea and Me.

      Of course, we're planning a quick wedding just before we cross the line into Canada so "Pop" can give her away before he returns. We'll probably be staying in a motel for a month or so until I find work. Bea doesn't think she'll have any trouble getting a nursing position, and I'm told they also have lots of cars in Canada - imagine that! So, I should fit right in somewhere, too - employment wise.

      If anyone asks you about either of us, just say the last you heard we were planning a short trip before I was due to report for basic training. Until further notice, we will only be communicating with Mr. Wood (Abner - can you believe that name?) and he'll send you our address as soon as we write to inform him we've left the motel.

      To my knowledge no one in Rosemont has ever done anything like this, so I don't know what, if any, reaction my "desertion" will cause. All I know is that I'm excited and happy, with no regrets except leaving you. It's probably too soon for you to make a drastic change for yourself, but maybe in a year or two you'll consider travelling north, too - as an honest adventurer, though, not a fugitive.

      Bea sends her greetings, and our puppy, Dodger, says "Arf."

Lots of love,

Dash

FIVE

The Wood residence on Westmoreland Avenue was set back about twenty yards from the sidewalk, so at night it received little benefit from the nearest streetlights. I had driven by the house in daylight about a week before and remembered it as large and white with black trim around the windows and having a spacious L-shaped porch. But tonight, after parking near the curb, all I could see was a shapeless black mass with a faint glow coming from an upstairs window. By now it was early November, and since I had heard nothing further from Dash or Abner Wood, I'd decided to pay a call, figuring that if no one answered my knock, though a station wagon sat in the driveway, then perhaps I'd phone Mr. Wood tomorrow. After walking confidently toward the front door and up three steps, I could just make out the tiny black button that must be the doorbell.

Before I had a chance to press it, however, a creaking sound hit my ear from the shadows next to me, where, with a shudder, I saw the seated figure of a man moving slowly back and forth on a suspended porch swing. The wide brim of one those fedora hats, that had recently become unfashionable for men, added to the natural camouflage of the dark night, so I saw not one detail of his face, even though he was within an arm's reach of me.

"Excuse me. I was just going to ring the bell." I felt like a lonely trick-or-treater, one who was just a few nights late.

"You with the IRS?" His voice was hushed and almost fearful.

"No, gee - of course not, sir." Yes, I did say "gee." And from in front of the face a cloud of smoke added another detail to the picture: he was a pipe smoker, and in a second the rich, pungent odor of his tobacco blew my way.

"My name is Jerry - Jerry Shifter. Your daughter, Bea - and Paul - I'm sure they mentioned me to you?"

"My little girl," he said. "My sweet little Beatrice Jane."

He quickly turned his head back out toward my car.

"I know a government car when I see one, young man."

"Mr. Wood, I'm not with the government. Aren't you cold out here, sir?"

"I don't get cold any more - not since this." He pointed to his forehead.

"Your hat," I said, "Yes, you need a hat on a cool night like this."

With a flashing gesture, he removed the hat and pointed to a bald patch of his scalp. I moved a few steps closer and saw, in a sliver of moonlight, his finger tracing the contour of a rough, crooked scar.

"You've had an operation?"

"Oh, have a seat - why don't you?"

Looking around, I saw no other chair, so I made a move to sit next to him on the glider. He pushed me away, with a surprisingly strong arm, back toward the door, and pointed to the top step.

"There, sit there, and turn this way so I can see you."

I did as I was told and managed to get a fleeting look at him before he replaced his hat. Expecting to see a withered husk of a face, I saw instead handsome features and sad, glistening eyes behind a pair of wire-rimmed glasses.

"Now, what is there about the course work that you don't understand, young man?"

Realizing what I was probably up against, I thought there was no reason not to simply forge ahead.

"Do you know how I can get in touch with Bea - Beatrice Jane and Paul?"

"They had to - SHE had to drive me back here."

"Bea drove you back from Canada? But she's gone back to him?"

"You must devote more time to your studies, Howard. A fine-looking athlete such as yourself needs a passing grade in this course, you know. You must get your brain in as good a shape as your body."

"I'll try to do better, sir, but do you have an address for your daughter in Canada?"

"It's right here," he said, tapping his head. "She put everything in here. She knew how to do it. Yes sir, she knew how to do it. Who would have thought a little girl could learn to do such things? Beatrice Jane always was full of surprises. And you can learn too, Howard, very easily - if you commit yourself to your studies. I can give you extra help."

"All I'd really like, professor, is Bea's address in Canada."

"Canada's much too far away, but if you'd take your shirt off you'd be more comfortable. . ."

He stopped swinging and leaned closer to me. I think he was smiling now. His remark about my shirt didn't even register. Holding the bowl of his pipe with two fingers, he worked his lips, making little sucking sounds that sounded like the clicking of some night insect.

"Now, we have to do our best to get your grades up so Coach McNulty will keep you on the team. But I'm not sure it was a good idea to come out here to the lake, Howard. Your skin is pale. We can't have you go home with a sunburn."

"Sunburn, Mr. Wood? Will you let me have their address - or phone number? I'd really like to talk to them."

"I'm going inside now to get the lotion. It will keep you from getting sunburn. I'll rub it all over you. I give very good massages, you know. There's no one else here on the beach but us, Howard. Yes, that's it - take your shorts off, too. I'll be back in a jiffy."

He stood up and quickly went inside for the lotion. I'm sure I was in my car speeding away long before he found it.

SIX

It must have been about a week later on a Sunday afternoon, just a few days before Thanksgiving, that I was finishing up one of Big Ed's meat loaf dinners at Drake's. When Emma took my order, she asked again if I'd heard from Dash. This time I let her know I was upset and that he had probably skipped town with his girlfriend. She'd heard from a friend who worked for the draft board that he never showed up for his physical, and that his case was being investigated. I acted as worried and troubled as I could, something easy for me to do.

At some point I looked up and saw the familiar face of Mrs. Drest coming into the diner with a man I at first presumed to be her husband, before quickly remembering she was a widow. I waved at her and she came directly toward me, pulling the man with her by her hand and grinning broadly.

"Oh, hello, Jeremy, what a treat to bump into you! This is my older brother, Dave."

He was the editor of the town's daily newspaper, the Rosemont Gazette. I indicated the empty space at my table for them to join me, but Mrs. Drest wouldn't dream of it.

"Dave and I are the first of our party to arrive. Our church choir is having a little supper here this evening in the dining room - our minister's birthday, you know. Dave and I are going to hang some decorations we brought in this afternoon. Why don't you join us after you've finished your dinner? You can have some of the chocolate cake Ed has baked for Reverend Stewart."

I found myself smiling broadly now as well, completely and pleasantly surprised at her cheery demeanor in this new book-deprived setting.

"Alright," I replied, "perhaps I will. Give me a few minutes, and I may just help you with the decorations."

As she dragged her brother along to the deserted dining room, I heard her say, "That's the darling young man I work with."

Five minutes later I was standing on a folding chair, helping her hang a Happy Birthday sign on the wall. Nearby, Dave and Emma were setting the tables for the group that would soon be arriving.

I thought I'd attempt, while I had the opportunity, to get more information from Mrs. Drest about Professor Wood.

"You know," I began, "I happened to meet Abner Wood the other night. His daughter - the one you met - was dating my good friend - "

A look of considerable alarm flooded her face, and she let her half, the "happy" half of the banner, fall.

"Haven't you heard?"

"Heard what?"

"About the fire. It's been on the radio all day. It'll be headlines in the Gazette tomorrow. Mr. Wood's home has burned down, killing him. The poor man!"

Shocked and taken aback - quite literally, I'm afraid, I lost my footing on the chair and fell to the floor. Big Ed, hearing the racket from the kitchen, came scrambling out and had me scooped up in his beefy arms and standing upright almost before I'd fully realized what happened. Mrs. Drest, amazed, stood frozen in disbelief, her arms extended toward me.

"Jeremy, dear, are you alright?"

I said I was just fine, thank you. Her brother gave a hearty laugh and said he hadn't heard her call anyone "dear" in a long time, and that I'd better be careful or one day soon SHE'D be falling for me.

I think Ed was relieved that one of his customers wouldn't need medical attention, and after sitting me down on the chair I'd tumbled from, returned with Emma to the kitchen, mumbling that "the Lutherans" were on their way in.

Somehow, I managed to be sociable and join in the festivities. Mrs. Drest drew me aside to ask me to please start calling her by her first name, Katherine, then introduced me playfully to their minister as her "Catholic colleague." We sang the birthday song, and Katherine removed her simple gray jacket, revealing a garish orange and black paisley-patterned blouse underneath. She joined the choir members - all eight of them - for the singing of two hymns. Reverend Stewart and his somber wife seemed suitably pleased, as was I, when it became clear he wasn't going to give anything like a speech. My thoughts kept drifting compulsively back to what I felt surely must be the charred ruin of Abner Wood's house and to what sort of Thanksgiving my friend Dash and his wife would soon be having.

Not long after the reverend and his wife left, Dave approached me for a little talk over one final cup of coffee in a corner of the dining room. I learned he'd been the editor of the paper for eleven years, and was married to "a treasure" named Connie. His sister's husband had been killed in action in Korea over a decade ago fighting for a piece of land the Army had named Pork Chop Hill. He hunched in closer to me and whispered that, confidentially, "the poor girl hasn't been able to cook or eat pork chops since." He was very easy to talk to, and soon approached the tricky subject that must have been uppermost in his mind all along.

He was going to trust me not to tell his sister that he had brought such a personal matter up, for she was a very private person and would never forgive him if she found out. It turns out she had often spoken favorably about me to both him and his wife at family dinners and informal visits this past year. On more than one occasion she had expressed a concern that I no doubt felt she was old enough to be my mother, adding that I always behaved very formally around her. I think my embarrassment began to show here, so he quickly got to the point.

"She's only thirty-six years old - how old are you, buddy?"

"Twenty-six," I replied.

He seemed overjoyed at the tidings.

"There you are!" he exclaimed. "Not that big an age difference at all. And one more thing - she's rather well off. Our father left us both a major inheritance when he passed away."

We both caught sight of her approaching from the exit, where she had been saying goodnight to some friends. She looked at us inquiringly as she came closer. Dave stood up and extended a hand to me.

"Hope to see you over the holiday season, Jeremy."

I helped Katherine slide into her gray jacket and the three of us, together, headed for the doorway. It seemed that in the past few minutes I'd been given much more to worry about than Dash, Bea and the smoking debris back on Westmoreland Avenue.

SEVEN

FORMER COLLEGE PROF. DIES IN HOUSE FIRE

The body of Abner Wood was found deceased in the rubble of the family home yesterday morning by firefighters responding to the three-alarm blaze on Westmoreland Avenue. No other bodies were found, though fire Chief Edward Slack expressed concern as to the whereabouts of the deceased's adult daughter, Beatrice, who is also listed as a resident at that address. The remains of several pets were found in cages in the former science instructor's basement laboratory.

Mr. Wood is known by many in Rosemont for his fifteen years of dedicated teaching at our college on South River Street. He left his position there a few years ago to pursue independent research and studies at his home

Chief Slack claims that he and Chief Garvin of Stroudsburg will be investigating the cause of the blaze that so quickly engulfed the structure. It is known that the homeowner smoked a pipe, but there is also a chance that the fire may have been caused by faulty electrical wiring on the premises.

****

A few days later I'd arranged to take some personal time off from the library in order to attend the graveside service of Abner's funeral. At first, I thought there might actually be a chance of seeing Bea, and even possibly Dash, at the cemetery. Although who, in either of their families, might have been able to contact them with the sad news of the fire, I had no idea. It was Katherine who finally convinced me not only to attend the funeral, but, once there, to tell someone in Mr. Wood's family what I knew concerning Dash's plan to travel with Bea to Canada to evade military service. She felt there was little chance that Dash and Bea could have heard any news about the tragedy. Dave told us he remembered one of his reporters had talked to Abner's sister when the paper ran a story about the professor's dismissal from the college a few years before. He recalled she lived in New York, and no doubt it was she who had been contacted to make the funeral arrangements.

We hadn't had any rain in weeks, so the layer of fallen leaves on the cemetery grounds was dry and crisp under the twenty or so sets of feet that walked from their parked cars on the nearby driveway toward the mound of recently dug earth under a slender birch tree. I thought the woman I had chosen to follow might well be Abner's sister. She seemed afraid of sliding on the dewy leaves and kept reaching out to the man accompanying her to steady herself, but he appeared oblivious of her needs. When we arrived at the designated spot, he turned to her, revealing one of those fish-like amphibian faces. Something about the way she carried herself suggested both poise and an awareness that almost anything might be on the verge of happening. When she did face me for a second, I saw a pale, attractive older woman with pink lipstick, her face crowned with a blond helmet of teased hair. I received an instant acknowledgment of some sort, but then she looked down, absorbed with re-arranging some bits of branches and leaves with her black patent leather shoes. In a few seconds we heard the minister, the very same one from Drake's the other night, begin the service.

Since most of the small crowd no doubt had attended the church service, they scattered rather quickly back to their cars as soon as the prayers ended. The woman next to me, however, continued to stand still with her companion.

"I get the impression you might have known my brother," she said.

I introduced myself and shook both their hands.

"I'm Abner's sister, Jane, and this is my husband, Larry. Were you a student of his?"

I told her I had only met her brother a few weeks ago, once, on the porch of his house. We stood there, only six or seven feet from the still exposed grave, and I told her everything: how I had met her niece at the library where I worked . . .

"The "Jane" part of her name is for me, you know. My Abner and I, we were so close as children."

. . . how after a few dates, we just didn't seem to hit it off, that there was something about her I found troubling . . .

"Even as a child, she was very strange. And we're so distraught about worrying where she might have gone, what's become of her. We've heard rumors from the undertaker that she was seeing someone - "

Here she grabbed hold of Larry's hand. I continued.

. . . how I introduced Bea to my life-long friend and they seemed to instantly click, and that just when they were really getting serious, Paul received his notice from the draft board.

"And you think that's why no one knows where she is? That she ran away with him?"

. . . how I phoned the hospital yesterday and talked to her nursing supervisor. No one there knew where she is, and that, yes, I felt fairly certain they'd made plans to cross the border into Canada a few weeks ago.

Jane turned to her husband and told him she still wanted to visit the chief of police, if not to file a missing person's report, then at least to tell him what they had heard from me.

I babbled on, like the real snitch I had become.

"I received a letter from Paul saying that your brother was going to follow them up in his own car, and that he had given them a good deal of money to help give them a start."

As soon as I said that, Larry piped up with a suggestion that they should head right to the bank and find out how much cash was left in Abner's account.

"Oh, Larry," she said, "that money is all hers now, regardless."

"Maybe not - now that they're practically fugitives - if what this kid says is - "

112

"Kid!" I nearly shouted, "I'm not a kid - I'm twenty-six. Anyway, the reason I went to see your brother last week was to find out if he had their new address, or just to see how they were when he left Canada. But your brother seemed. . . sort of confused, almost disoriented. He even showed me a scar on his head - like here."

I gestured to the spot just above my ear and asked if she knew anything about a recent operation he might have had.

She shook her head back and forth repeatedly.

"No, no, no, we haven't kept in touch now for years, not since Beatrice Jane was six or seven - after Abner's wife died we had a falling out -"

Larry was getting steamed again.

"Jane, for god's sake, you don't have to blab the family history, do you?"

"This gentleman is worried about his friend and my niece, Larry, and I think you can at least loosen up a bit and try to be civil."

Then, to me.

"My husband and I are both New Yorkers, you see, and don't know quite how to behave in this quaint small town."

Jane took hold of my elbow and drew me aside a little, her husband walking just ahead of us.

She and Abner had been born in Manhattan on the upper west side in a lovely apartment on Riverside Drive. Their father was a veterinarian, who also operated a very swanky kennel or boarding facility for the pets of some of the city's wealthiest animal lovers, people who liked to take pet-free vacations abroad. When she spoke of this as we walked slowly back to our cars, with Larry three steps ahead, I made a connection with the animal remains and cages at the fire scene.

"Abner was going to be a vet," she continued, "in fact he studied to be one, but one of his teachers encouraged him to go into pre-med. That's how he got involved with Biology as a major, but he just couldn't see himself as a doctor. And then he met a pretty young nurse - Beatrice Jane's poor mother - "

Here she stopped both of us in our tracks near her car, in which Larry already sat frowning behind the wheel. Behind the windshield, he looked, I thought, exactly like some new species of fish in an aquarium.

Jane lowered her voice to a whisper now.

"She committed suicide, stole poison from the hospital. She left two- TWO, mind you - suicide notes, one for the police and one for Abner and Beatrice Jane."

I decided to ask one rather impertinent question.

"Have you any idea why he was asked to leave his position at Rosemont College?"

She replied surprisingly quickly, as if it were the most inconsequential matter imaginable.

"Oh, it had something to do with those experiments he was doing on animals. With Abner it was always animals, you know. Ever since he was a child. And Beatrice Jane shared - grew to share all her father's interests."

She turned on a bright smile, we said good-bye, and they drove out of my life as quickly as they had entered it.

EIGHT

During that entire holiday season and the unusually mild winter that followed, Katherine and I began to see a great deal of each other - so much so that we felt we might be overdoing it. We would spend nearly every day on the job together, our schedules often identical, and then we'd go out in the evening for dinner, drinks at the Carousel out on Highway 6, or to a movie. On one of these evenings, she confided in me that sex wasn't really that important to her, and that she felt there were other ways we could "share intimacies." I pretended to be shocked, as if everything we'd been doing, or in this case NOT doing, was normal.

We were driving, parked somewhere actually, and she was looking at me - her eyes cast down below the steering wheel, where yet again, nothing was stirring.

"I can help you to use your hands, Jeremy. You can touch me, and we can take our time. You know I'm practically too old to have children anyway, so I don't want you to feel any sort of pressure about any of this. It's certainly no reason for us to stop seeing each other, is it? Especially when we enjoy being together so much. and it's certainly wonderful to have found someone, isn't it?"

Speechless. I sat there speechless.

She was crying, softly, so softly, as though she were becoming someone I'd never seen before. In the shadows of the car I thought I might be looking at the girl she once was, the little Katie I never had the chance to know. The soldier's girl. Suddenly I was overcome with a rush of feelings for her, not passion certainly, but a sense that she understood things about me that even I had trouble acknowledging myself. She was opening herself up so completely that I knew if I were to fail her regarding this issue, I would probably never find anyone else who would allow me to take this sort of leap again.

I inched closer to her across the front seat, and she took my hand, raised my fingers to her lips, kissed them and placed them on the inside of her thigh. She leaned back, sighing, as both of us began what was, for me at least, a very new phase of life.

********** **********

It was the middle of March, not long before Easter, when Dave and his wife invited us over for dinner and a birthday celebration for their sixteen-year-old daughter, Irene. Katherine and I thought it would be a good time to announce that we were officially engaged and considering a wedding in August. Irene good-naturedly charged us with trying to upstage her big day with our announcement but did seem genuinely touched by the gift of money we gave her. Connie, Dave's wife, had baked a delicious chocolate cake, topped with sixteen candles that shed the usual glow when Dave switched off the dining room light. We sang the song, cheering when Irene blew her candles out.

"So much to celebrate tonight," said Dave.

"We'd better be careful," replied Connie, "or Dave will use your wedding announcement as the headlines in tomorrow's Gazette."

A little later, while the women cleared and started washing the dishes, Dave and I went into the little room he referred to as his "refuge," where he had a pair of large, fully stacked book cases, two comfortable chairs and a stereo console with built-in radio. There was also a desk with one of those electric typewriters on top. The first thing he did, after motioning for me to sit down, was to open the window and light up a cigarette.

"You know," he said before sitting down across from me, "this is a great thing you're doing. A really great thing. Kate's happiness means the world to me. You have no idea."

I told him I thought I did, adding that my folks in Allentown were just as surprised and happy for me. Katherine had met them a few weeks before, and they could easily tell how serious we were about each other.

"But you and Connie are the first ones we've actually mentioned the wedding to."

"I only wish she'd met you a few years earlier, for your sake, Jeremy. You know - so you two could have children together."

"Gee, Dave," I said, feeling a bit astonished at his frankness, "that's just not an issue for us, you know."

"Great that you both see it that way. And you could, of course, always adopt a kid."

"Yes," I replied, trying my best to sound agreeable, "but that would be our decision. Married couples do exist without children."

"Indeed," he said, "it's not unheard of." He inhaled a pointedly large amount of Marlboro fumes. "The whole business of baby-making is probably overrated. Look at Connie and me - we only managed one!"

He laughed, but it sounded forced, so he quickly added that Irene was really a sweetie, wasn't she?

"You know," he said, gesturing toward one of his books on a nearby shelf, "in ancient times, like in Greece and Rome, all kinds of sexual things we think of as immoral today were going on regularly."

"I just don't see the connection," I said. And I didn't.

Somewhat flustered, he went on. "Well, I mean we were talking about baby-making, weren't we?"

"Yes, we were, but these immoral things - I'm assuming you're referring to homo - "

He laughed again. "Of course, you and Kate are both educated librarians! You would both know all about these historical matters - all I'm suggesting is that . . ."

Here he managed the tricky maneuver, without once getting up, of forcing his chair a few inches closer to me by shifting his body weight on the cushion, and digging his heels into the carpet, moving forward as though he were in a wheel chair.

"You must go through a lot of chairs that way, Dave"

I don't think he found my remark amusing but seemed eager to return to his topic.

" . . . such behaviors are much more common today than most people realize, Jeremy. Don't you think?"

"I suppose so."

"Bi-sexuality, for example, is a fascinating custom, don't you think? Take the Beatles, for instance."

"You think they're bi-sexual?"

"Oh, their hair, their bangs - that's the giveaway. And all these hippies with their long hair. It's all coming back into fashion, you see - they're even calling it the sexual revolution."

"You wouldn't be testing out your next editorial on me, would you?"

Flashing a devilish grin that was almost a leer, he reached out and put his large hand a few inches above my knee and gave my leg a good squeeze. He was far too clever to leave it there for long, though.

"Yes, it's going to be wonderful having a guy like you in the family - looking forward to many great talks here, Jeremy. I feel I can speak my mind to you, and sure hope you feel that way too, Jerry - may I call you Jerry? I think I've heard Kate call you that, haven't I?"

"Yes," I replied, "of course you can call me Jerry."

"Brothers, then, soon to be?"

"Brothers."

********** **********

A few weeks later Katherine and I were in her apartment sitting at her table making a list of the people we'd be inviting to the wedding. At some point she noticed my interest had faded and was no longer focused.

"Wait a minute, what's wrong? It's like you're no longer here."

'I was thinking about how - ordinarily I'd be sure to invite Dash, that's all."

She read even much more than that in my face as well.

"It's been a while since you've talked about those two. He probably would have been your best man as well."

"Oh, yeah - that's for sure."

Then, a stunner began to brew.

"I want you to know I haven't kept this from you for long. I only found out about it today. You saw me take that lengthy call today in my office?"

"I figured it was something to do with the book orders."

"It was Susan Floss."(Her source at the university.)

"I like Susan. How's she doing?"

"She heard that Bea's back - not here in Rosemont, though. Susan's friend saw her in Stroudsburg, bumped into her at the train station."

"And Dash?"

"They broke up - separated or something. Bea told Susan's friend she found a note on the motel bed one morning saying he was sorry but that he was leaving to try to start off on his own. He left the car with her, said he bought a bus ticket and planned to get lost or something. Took some of Abner's money with him but left the rest for her."

"Anything else?" My voice was suddenly hoarse.

"Bea's on a hospital nursing staff out there around Stroudsburg somewhere. They never did get married, honey."

"And did you get the idea they had already made it as far as Canada when he left?"

"I've got Susan's number here. You can talk to her yourself if you want."

"Maybe - maybe not."

"Oh, for silly's sake - you're not angry at me for not telling you earlier, are you?"

I was tapping my fingers repeatedly on the table cloth, a nervous habit, I'm sure. It began to remind me of Morse code, and as soon as it did, I stopped doing it.

NINE

It was a pleasant spring afternoon, maybe two weeks later, when I took an invigorating fast walk over to Drake's for my lunch break. When I got inside I could see Dave getting up from the counter and hoped he would continue his exit, so I wouldn't have to spend the next half hour with him. No such luck. Seeing me caused his 'public smile', as Kate called it, to light up his face.

"Good excuse for me to have another cup of coffee. The counter okay for you?"

I thought two could play this stupid social game, so, managing a smile of my own, I sat on the adjacent stool and gave Emma my order. I made a mental note to remind Kate to add her to our wedding invitation list before finalizing it.

Because the journalist in him was never far beneath the surface, his first words were a direct plea for information.

"Any word from your missing friends yet?"

I wasn't exactly eager to unload my anxieties on him but thought doing so might at least spare Kate from having to listen to more of my whining tonight.

"No, and what's upsetting is that if he had any family, they'd be the ones making the inquiries on his behalf. I'd be regarded as 'only his friend.' "

"Yes, and him being a draft dodger adds to the complications, Jeremy. There's that, too."

I asked Emma to bring me a grilled cheese with tomato and to put "the editor's" extra coffee on my bill.

"And there's something about that fire still worries me," I said.

"You gotta understand, though, that from an outsider's point of view, all we got is a dead guy in a house fire - no sign of arson either, by the way. Five years ago, he lost his job - so what? His daughter's boyfriend's a draft dodger - so a guy who deserts his country, deserts her, too. What we need is connections, someone or something to connect the dots. Now Kate tells me she heard the daughter's surfaced as a nurse in Stroudsburg, right?"

"Yeah, that's what she heard - from a woman who used to know Bea's dad at the college."

"Well, there's a chance your buddy will surface one of these days, too. Does he have your phone number?"

"Yes, I even wrote it down for him and gave it to him the last time I saw him."

"Be sure not to change it when you move into your new digs after the big event in August. Ma Bell might charge a slight fee to do that, but you don't want to make things even more complicated for the guy."

Emma brought my grilled cheese, adding that good food is like good sex - it leaves you wanting seconds. Then she cast a wicked glance at Dave.

"Just ask your wife, Dave."

"That Emma -she's something else, isn't she?" he said as she walked away.

"She sure is," I said." But she's really a good-hearted girl."

"Her husband," he added, lowering his voice, "must have quite a tool in his tool box to keep her happy, right?"

I might have nodded my head while working on my sandwich. He went back to our original subject.

"No, the way I see it, you'd be better off, for your own psychological peace of mind, if you just put those two old friends of yours out of your head. You and Kate have more important and happier things on the horizon, right?"

He was getting up now, starting to leave, but not before placing a friendly hand on my shoulder.

"I hear more than a little bit of Kate in that advice, Dave."

"Oh,' he said, "she and I have a lot in common, that's for sure."

***** ****** ***** *****

It was only a few days later that Kate came into the library to begin her night shift work schedule. I was always happy to see her enter through the doors on these afternoons because it meant I would be leaving in just another hour. I would have a few hours to myself before dropping by her apartment. I saw right away that she was carrying a large manila envelope under her arm, which she handed to me before entering her office.

"Here's a present for you," she said.

"It feels like paper. Hope it's money," I replied.

She told me Dave had left this morning for a journalism workshop in Philadelphia and would be gone for the rest of the week. She had just come from the Gazette building and, specifically, Dave's office and the cabinet in which she knew he kept old, partially completed, or unused articles from the past few years. She had a pretty good idea she'd find some reporter's notes on the Abner Wood dismissal.

"Well," I said, "I can't decide whether you'd like to moonlight as a woman reporter or a woman detective. Which is it?"

"I feel more like a cat burglar," was her reply. "But I do worry that I'm adding to your obsession. I just skimmed the few papers quickly. Read them as soon as possible, will you? Take some notes if you want, I should return them tonight after my shift's over. Though I can't imagine he'll ever miss them. I remember the reporter - his name was Dawes, and he took a job offer in Los Angeles about a year and a half ago. He and Dave were sort of close for a while - you know how guys are, right? I do agree with him that there's not much to go on, though."

"Thanks, Kate." I was genuinely touched by the risk she'd taken to perhaps provide some relief for me from the mood of depression that she'd been observing in me for weeks now.

"I know I haven't been good company lately, but this means a lot, honey," and I started to move closer.

"There's to be no affectionate displays in the library, young man, you know that."

Her lilac scent rushed by me, transporting me really, but she quickly became serious and thoughtful.

"Still," she mused, "I can't help but think Dash would have written you or called you by now. And you say he's an only child with both parents out of the picture?"

"Right."

"So, once he left the girl, it's like you're all he has left?"

"You could say that, yes."

********* *********

The reporter's name was Frank Dawes, and what looked like a high school yearbook photo of his head and shoulders was clipped to the four typed papers Kate had pieced together from the original notes. The young Dawes looked smart behind his black rimmed glasses, head turned slightly camera right, smiling slightly, with a head of wavy hair slicked back, greaser style.   He had first visited Bea in the cafeteria of St. Luke's Hospital where she was in her first year of employment as a nurse. Her father had lost his job at Rosemont College just a week before.

Frank's informal notes had obviously been hastily written, filled with abbreviations and difficult to decipher. Bea had no doubt been seated directly across from him during the interview: "looks young but acts older, nervous, hesitant . . . says Dad's a good man and doesn't want more publicity. . . would be angry if he knew she was answering personal questions . . . clear she's very upset at the way college is treating him. Research is his life, as much as he enjoys teaching, it's the research that's the thing for him . . . thinks students complained about things they saw in the lab or something . . . feels he wasn't given the chance to defend himself . . . doesn't talk to her much about the experiments he does in the labs, she knows he received a grant for his research . . . the funding had ended . . . he's not worried about finances . . . thinks that money-wise they're okay . . . experiments she thinks have to do with animals, mostly mice, she thinks. . . "little critters, you know, maybe rabbits" . . . Dad grew up in Manhattan . . .. grandpa was a veterinarian . . . a guy named Neil Perth is the chairman of Rosemont's Science department, thinks I should talk to him . . . she wants her dad to get a lawyer . . . says work he's doing will one day benefit - blah, blah - flirting with me now, loosening up . . . dad is so determined to continue under terrible pressure . . . both are anxious . . . enjoys nursing, it's easy, everyone treats her fine . . . says I look strong, what sports do I play?. . . . . she's sort of cute . . . abrupt switch back to a rage against the students who complained . . . says if I talk to any of them . . . shouldn't listen to them . . . says Perth is a real nitwit . . .I wouldn't want her for MY nurse . . . mouth moves in twisty directions when she chews her french fries . . . can't tell me much about the experiments - something about animal behavior. . . altering their tendencies, impulses. . . she herself hardly listens to him when he talks about it . . . he's really obsessed, she thinks . . . still lives at home with him, doesn't pay rent but wants to move out soon . . . do I want her phone number . . . do I?

Kate had inserted a note here, stating someone had typed two phone conversations Dawes recorded three days after the above meeting with Bea. They were calls to Dr. Neil Perth, Abner's immediate supervisor, who had held the position of chairman of the science department for ten years. Prior to that he'd seen action on the beaches of Normandy for which he received a purple heart.

CONVERSATION 1:
N.P.   Dr. Perth here - Good morning.
F.D.   Hello Doctor, Frank Dawes here from the Rosemont Gazette. I think I was talking to your secretary yesterday. She said this might be a good time to have a brief chat with you about a story we plan to run in the paper one of these days.
N.P   Yeah, though I can't imagine anything we do here is even remotely newsworthy.
F.D.   The college dismissed one of your department's instructors a couple of weeks ago.
N.P.   You're referring to Abner Wood?
F.D.   Yes.
N.P.   And?
F.D.   I was wondering what you can tell me about the circumstances.
N.P.   You just SAID all I care to discuss about it: the college did indeed dismiss one of the science instructors, Abner Wood. That's it.
F.D.   His family is thinking about hiring a lawyer. I thought you might be willing to share some information as to a reason or reasons for the college taking such action - especially in the middle of a semester.
N.P.   Even if I did know the reason, I would not be at liberty to reveal it. You might have more luck talking to Dean Davenport, though I doubt it.
F.D.   A source tells me a complaint was lodged by one of his students. I -
N.P.   Four.

F.D.   What?

N.P.   There, that's my one contribution to your story, and I give you that only because I subscribe to your paper, enjoy doing the crossword puzzle and reading the comics. Good-bye

CONVERSATION #2

N.P.   Hello.

F.D.   Dr. Perth?

N.P.   Yes, who is this?

F.D.   Frank Dawes again, from the Gazette.

N.P.   Calling me at home now? This seems -

F.D.   You do understand that even on the slim chance there is something worth publishing regarding this story - and I'll be honest with you, Doctor, I really don't think there will be, I would only refer to you as "a source at the college." Your name would not be used. Now you mentioned something about the complaints of four students. I was wondering if it could be a matter concerning their grades in a course? Or if -

N.P.   No, no, no, it wouldn't be anything like that - especially with him. Always gave high grades easily.

F.D.   Sounds like that's probably not true for you, eh, Doc? I'd no doubt have to struggle hard to pass your course.

N.P.   That's what makes this affair so hard for us here, Mr. Dawes. He was a very popular instructor until this matter came up. It seemed to come out of the blue in a way. There didn't seem to be any reason for him to expose the students to the work he was doing on his own in his lab experiments. Some very bright, level-headed students- two of them have some real clout in this town- oh, goodness, I shouldn't say any more.

F.D. I did hear someone mention laboratory animals - mice or rabbits - were they being abused in some way? Was that it?

N.P.   More than mice and rabbits - it was the fact that he talked to his students about his theories. Ideas come cheaply you know, they're a dime a dozen. I told him repeatedly I couldn't believe he'd been given a grant to pursue such harebrained - there's a rabbit word for your crossword puzzle, young man - such ridiculous notions.

F.D.   Was it something to do with changing the behavior of animals?

N.P.   Who have you been talking to? Of course, it was HOW he intended to achieve that - that was the thing - he's a brilliant man, a very brilliant man. And he claimed he was close to a breakthrough . . .

F.D.   And so, I guess he couldn't keep it to himself and started blabbing about his ideas in class one day.
N.P.   More to it, Dawes, more to it than that. I must say good-bye now. (LONG PAUSE)
          . . . Don't call again.

****** ****** ******

That very night I took Kate up on her offer and did indeed phone Susan Floss. Using whatever combination of charm and guile I may have possessed in those days, I succeeded in getting her to reveal the name of one of the students to whom Dr. Perth must have alluded.

Susan had been none other than Neill Perth's personal secretary through the entire time the department scandal (there really is no other word to describe the academic consternation at the highest levels of the college in those days) was occurring. Miss Floss knew the young man well; it seemed nearly everyone on campus did. He was not only an excellent scholar and captain of the Groundhogs, the college baseball team, but more to the point - his father owned much valuable real estate throughout the county. In short, a young man whose annoyance regarding a professor was not to be taken lightly. And then, of course, three others came forth.

Donald Janker, that was the name, had graduated by this time and was still in town doing some paralegal work at the law firm that represented his family's business affairs. Susan also happened to know that he tended bar at Sandy's Tavern on River Road on Thursday and Friday nights. I planned to pay a visit there on the first Thursday that rolled along.

TEN

Long and lean as a pitcher should be, he seemed to tower over the bar at which I was only one of four patrons: one guy at each end and another two stools to my right, noisily cracking a peanut every few seconds. Tony Bennet was complaining that he had left his heart in San Francisco, which did little to enliven the rather somber little group. No more than four couples sat at the booths, so I thought it might be easy to engage Janker in a friendly chat.

"Say, didn't you pitch for the Groundhogs a few years ago?"

"You bet, buddy," and down he came with a bowl of peanuts. "We won the class "B" champ trophy the year I graduated."

"You're - wait a minute - Janker, aren't you?"

"Can't believe you remember my name."

"What I really remember is that I was dating a girl at the time who graduated from Rosemont a few years before. She was sort of what they call an alumnus - wanted to go see you pitch - think she was hot for you, mister."

Actually blushing, with a shy smile, he said something I didn't quite hear.

"What?"

"I said 'alumna' with an "A" - that's the feminine ending - Latin, you know."

"You must have had some good Latin prof there, right?"

''Yeah, we had some first-rate instructors at Rosemont. What can I get you?"

"A double bourbon, two ice cubes."

Fifteen seconds and he was back with it, still wearing his college ring wrapped around a long thick finger.

"A shame about that college prof who died in that house fire some months back, wasn't it? What was his name?"

"Old Woody, a first-class nutcase."

"I always thought he seemed like a sensible enough fella, but then they fired him or maybe he quit - I don't know."

"No, you hit it right the first time. They canned him."

I felt like a prospector about to strike a vein of gold.

"Was he messin' around with one of the girls in his class?"

"Nothin' that normal. I was in his class - "

"Science?"

"Bio - So, one day in class he starts talking about this theory he's got, right?"

"Yeah?"

"Says scientists, medical guys, have no idea what entire sections of the human brain can do. Imagine, he said, what you could do if you could cut away - surgically, you know - just a tiny slice of human brain tissue from one of these areas, one of these areas that are like - inactive, and then implant that sample - graft it into or onto an animal's brain. Said you could probably create a whole race of animals that would have extraordinary capabilities. Can . . . you . . . fucking . . . believe it?"

"Looks like we had our very own mad scientist right here under our noses, I guess."

"Wait," Janker said, "it gets better. He goes on to say he's been doing experiments, but that his real stumbling block is how to find someone willing to let him cut into their brain!"

"No chance he was joking?"

"Hell, no, man! So, some of us crack up laughing at this point, and he flips out and starts screaming, saying that this is his life's work. I don't mind talking about all this cause he's dead now, so it can't do any harm anymore. Then he points to me - ME - and says he'd pay a hundred dollars if I'd allow him to cut a small slice - a "brain shaving", that's the term he used. He said if any of us would agree to the harmless surgery, we, along with him, would make medical history."

I said something about the whole thing sounding like a bad science fiction movie.

"Again, there's more - after class he takes a few of us down the hall to his private lab where he does his experiments. So, he shows us his little zoo, you know - five or six cages with bunny rabbits, mice and even a couple of frogs, and every one of them looked sick as hell. And almost all of them had these little cuts and scars on their heads.

I'm sure one of the rabbits was dead. You sure downed that drink fast. Want another?"

"Affirmative," I said, handing him the glass. I sat there with a vivid memory of the creepy scar Abner had showed me on his own scalp. By the time Donald returned with my second bourbon, however, I thought he must have regretted his loose lips because he switched gears and asked me if I followed baseball. So, we talked about the Yankees and the Phillies for a while, and my neighbor, Mr. Peanut, asked for another beer. Just when I thought my fount of information had dried up, back he headed in my direction, wiping the slick surface of the bar with a damp sponge. Leaning in kind of quietly, he whispered in my ear.

"Just between you and me, pal, I know for a fact old Woody liked to take a walk on the other side of the street now and then. Know what I mean?"

"Yeah, I guess I do."

"So, the guy was really messed up, was a regular customer at the Peach Tree. Know the place?"

"Well, yes, I've heard about it."

It was the only gay bar anywhere near Rosemont, located in Scranton, about twenty miles away.

Janker felt the need to add a few more choice comments.

"My dad has a lot of connections, see, so a businessman friend of his says the professor often used to be seen at the Peach Tree with another one of our local celebrities."

I had to ask, naturally, and received a quick response.

"The editor of the Gazette, Dave Chalmers."

I have no idea how my face must have altered at that news, but he sure noticed something about my reaction because he began babbling about how his boss was always telling him he talked "too goddamn much" to the customers. He sure hoped the editor wasn't a relative of mine, and I assured him he needn't worry. Then he asked me where I worked. When I told him, he smiled and said that explained why I looked so shocked.

"Librarians," he said, "you guys sure do live in another world. You ought to get with the hippies, man. They're on the right path."

I left him a dollar tip and tried, perhaps a little too hard, to strut as confidently and deliberately as I could manage out onto the dark streets.

In addition to all the news about Dr. Wood, I had also discovered why my future brother-in-law would no doubt never dig any further into matters relating to his deceased friend. And as I continued the long walk home that night, my mental image of Dash's face became suddenly dim and much harder for me to picture.

It was as if he were fading away into the darkness somewhere, beyond my ability to see him.

ELEVEN
THREE YEARS LATER

We named the baby Alice because we both loved Lewis Carroll's wonderful book. Though she didn't exactly look like his creation, for she was, we were pretty sure, half Vietnamese - no doubt the biological daughter of an American serviceman and his brown-skinned girlfriend. We were told that days after her birth she was brought to a Red Cross truck which transported her to an agency that had contacts with a Lutheran ministry. Kate's minister, **Reverend Warren Stewart**, had been on the lookout for our needs. Just a few weeks after officiating at our wedding, our Reverend Stewart was notified of her history and location. He began a series of phone calls that, surprisingly soon, resulted in our frantic flight to Los Angeles, where we got to hold her for the first time.

It was late summer, and we looked forward to spending the entire week of our vacation from the library in a cottage belonging to our new friends, the Millers, who were on a month-long trip to Europe. The little house was a lakefront property with its very own dock and rowboat, though no sooner had we seen the latter than we quickly agreed not to risk exposing Alice to the admittedly slight risk a gentle boat ride might involve. We decided, instead, to spend mostly every afternoon lying in the sun on a small strip of sandy public beach, just a short walk from the house. So, it was there we found ourselves, my wife, my daughter and I, on that Wednesday afternoon of August 7, 1971.

Kate and Alice were down the beach a little way from me, both involved in shaping small lumps of sand into a structure of some sort. This first shift with Alice, we had negotiated this morning over breakfast, would be Kate's; the second hour, after lunch, was to be mine. So, I lay face down on our large family beach blanket, wearing my dark blue speedo and reading our copy of THE GODFATHER - Kate was further along in it than I. It's really incredible how many details I can recall about that hour or, so we spent there that day. For example, the blanket was, by accident, also dark blue, the very same shade as my swim trunks. When Kate saw me lying there as she and Alice began walking away with their tin pails for sand, little shovels and a thermos of lemonade, she said I looked like I didn't have a middle. I remember laughing.

Early that morning, before we went out to Harker Lake, I told Kate she was exhibiting a more developed sense of humor after our wedding than she had ever showed before.

"That's because I finally got what I wanted," was her reply.

One of Alice's squeals distracted me from Vito Corleone's dilemmas and made me look up to check on my girls. That's when I saw, standing not far from them, the woman in the pink belted beach jacket, sunglasses and pink floppy hat with white polka dots. She held a long leather leash in her hand, and the other end of it was fastened to the collar of a big German Shepherd. I saw both of them in profile, both staring intently out at the shimmering lake and bathers.

Even before they turned to walk closer toward me, I'd recognized both of them: Bea and - yes, even the dog's name came back to me - Dodger.

She looked my way for a while, but behind those glasses I couldn't tell if she was staring at me. Then she adjusted them up onto her forehead, and I noted she was still wearing those crazy bangs she had on the day I first saw her.

"Mr. Jeremy Shifter," she said, smiling only faintly.

"Bea," trying to sound cheerful.

No doubt noticing the large, mostly vacant towel under me, she asked if I was here alone. I tilted my head toward the direction just behind her.

"My wife - you might know her - and my daughter, Alice."
She turned quickly.

"The girl in the yellow - oh, but isn't the child Chinese?"

"That's what nearly everyone says. No, she's Vietnamese - half, that is. You see, Kate and I adopted her."

"Oh, that's so nice."

Her dark shades fell back down into place.

"But no, I don't recognize the woman."

"You knew her as Mrs. Drest."

"You mean that other librarian?"

"Yes."

"Here," she said, tossing the end of the leash on my towel, "you keep an eye on him while I go over and introduce myself to your family. And I thought I was going to be bored here today - my husband is on the lake in his motorboat somewhere, fishing."

Her legs were still chubby and pale, so this was no doubt her first time out in the summer sun. Mine were just as white, like two trunks of ivory stretched out in front of me, the end of the leash next to them on my blanket. Dodger, lying next to me, looked listless and old before his time. The lively friskiness I remembered from the pet store had vanished.

"Poor kid," I spoke softly, stroking his black and gray head around his ear, and he nuzzled closer to my bare stomach.

It was then I noticed the scar, a ragged pink line about an inch long where hair would not grow. In my mind I heard the creaking of the swing on Abner's front porch, and the voice as well: "Who would have thought a little girl could learn to do such things?" I must have stared into the dog's eyes for a while, those sad, thoughtful eyes that people, somehow, just can't quite duplicate. Fearful thoughts, not sad ones, raced in a jumble through my mind.

Above me, it was Kate's voice that broke the spell of the nightmare.

"Alice and I are going for an ice cream. You and Bea can chat for a while, then I think we can go home early, okay?"

"Sure thing," I said, and the next thing I knew, the floppy pink hat, bangs and dark glasses were planted inches from me on the blanket. She had roughly lifted the animal before sitting and was now unfastening the leash's clip from its collar.

"I think he'll be fine just romping around here, don't you?"

"If you think he won't bother anyone."

"Him - he's such a gentle soul. Even my husband likes him - says he wishes I could be trained to lick his face the way Dodger does."

"It's easy to be nice to dogs, they never ask anything or expect anything of us. Sometimes we have high expectations of people, Bea. It's people who can be tricky that way, don't you think?"

"Well, haven't you become quite the philosopher! Is that what marriage has done to you?"

I figured my time with her would soon be coming to an end, so it would be ridiculous not to ask a few urgent questions.

"Whatever did happen to Dash?"

She turned from gazing at the dog, who was nosing around some rocks near the water's edge, to face me.

"A girl doesn't like talking about the guy who walked out on her, Jeremy."

"He loved you, Bea - hell, he was wacky over you. What happened?"

"The wacky part won over, I suppose." She tilted her head up at the blue sky at some birds screeching above us. "They look like gulls, but this is a lake." Then she must have realized I deserved at least another detail. "Oh, we met some motorcycle gang outside of Niagara, and Paul hit it off with them. They were only staying around the Falls for a couple of days, then they had plans to cross over into Canada. One of them had his wife along, and she had her own bike, but another one was riding one of those bikes that have a second seat attached alongside - and I think Paul talked the guy into taking him along."

I wondered if I should confront her with Susan Floss' story about his plans to take a bus trip, then thought maybe she had a right to tell a lie or two regarding such an embarrassing situation.

"So, what - he just rode off into the sunset with a biker gang?"

"Oh, there was more to it. We did have some fights, of course. Daddy was next door to us in an adjoining room. The trip north had taken a lot out of him. It wasn't easy. We were all getting anxious, you know . . . my, my, my, it looks as though Dodger has found something that interests him."

Down by the rocks, the dog's tail was swinging like mad while his dark, narrow snout seemed determined to sniff out something in the sand. I figured Bea was too eager to use him as an excuse to change the subject.

"Probably some insect or beetle trying to avoid being his snack. When did your father have that operation?"

The sunglasses came off in a flash, and that familiar twisted grimace she used those few times I watched her chew, worked over her mouth.

"Operation? What are you talking about?"

"He showed me his scar, Bea."

"He SHOWED you! When did you ever see him?"

"I went over to your house - I guess it was about a month after the three of you left - to try and get a phone number or address so I could write or call. But your dad was confused - at first, I thought he'd been drinking, but then I saw he was disoriented, didn't seem to know where he was. And then he showed me the scar on his bald head."

"Oh, he had a growth removed, but that was years ago. Paul noticed a change in him those last days too, before I drove him home. He must have gotten worse after he came home. You must have seen him shortly before the fire?"

"About a week before. And I met your aunt at the funeral."

"Jane? You met Aunt Jane!"

We both heard Dodger barking. As soon as he saw us looking his way, he resumed his curious duty, shoving his face with thrusting motions into the moist sand, tail still wagging.

"Bea, where do you think Dash is? What's become of him? There are all these crazy rumors about why your father had to leave the college. . . "

"You've been talking to ignorant shitheads, Jeremy - people with a Rosemont mentality, who wouldn't know a genius if - if he were living in their own back yard!"

Her last words were shouted as she got up with the leash. Brushing imaginary sand from her jacket, she took a tissue from her pocket and wiped what could have been a few real tears from her eyes.

I stood up, sensing our visit was ending.

"Bea - "I said, helpless and at a loss.

"Look, Jeremy, don't worry about Paul. I mean he's okay, I'm sure. He's alive somewhere. I may have done some awful things in my life - "

She pulled the shades off and stared defiantly right at me.

"- but I am NOT a murderer! - Dodger, come here, boy!"

The dog just stood there, staring back at us and barking.

"Bea, I never meant to . . . "

"Look, I know you two were best friends, but I'M the one he walked out on, and frankly, I don't think it's healthy for you to feel that strongly about another guy."

She was calming down now, re-adjusting her glasses and tightening her pink belt. She had a few more things to say.

"I like to think he joined up with those bikers, maybe found a gal of his own to ride with him along those cold Canadian roads. We saw a lot of drugs up there in those parts, that's for sure. Drugs are gonna be the way to go for all of us one day. Meanwhile, he'll get along - I'm sure he'll still be able to work on cars or fix their bikes - even if he's not quite the same fella you knew, Jeremy. He's changed by now, I think. I can see him as a brand-new Paul . . . but in a way, it's like part of him stayed behind with me . . . Dodger!"

The German Shepherd heard the harsh command and, tail between its legs, advanced slowly across the sand, zig-zagging around sunbathers, toward us.

"Come on, boy, we're gonna find the old man."

"Old man?" I asked.

"Yeah, that's what I call him. Isn't that funny - we both married old people, Jeremy. Good-bye - nice meeting the three of you."

Dodger startled me by looking up at me and barking. Even though distracted by the things she had just said, I reached down and scratched behind his pointed velvety ears.

"Good-bye, Bea." But she had already turned away.

They started for the parking lot, while I picked up my book and began to fold the beach blanket. Then, and still to this day I don't know why, I glanced out toward those rocks where Dodger had been poking around in the sand. I walked toward the general area, noting the crowd had increased in the last half hour. In the distance I heard the clickety-clack of the ascending roller coaster at Harker's Amusement Park on the other side of the lake. A few seconds later the thrilling screams of the riders as they plummeted, and one nearby toddler asking his mom if they could ride the coaster before going home. In a few years Alice might be ready for her first coaster ride, but certainly not yet. Now . . . just what had Dodger been pawing at on this part of the beach?

I walked around the recently scraped sand and looked down.

I'm not really sure, but I don't think I screamed. One short word made most likely by snout and paw, three letters in the damp, grainy crunched earth: DOT.

I turned away instantly, looked out at swimmers, splashers, sprays of water and playful shouts all along the lake. Maybe I hadn't seen it, maybe it was just another long-buried neurosis rearing its ugly head to torment me, this time on a beautiful summer day. When I finally got the courage to look again, the letters in the sand were still there.

Getting down on my knees seemed appropriate, like a worshipper at an ancient temple or a pilgrim viewing a sacred relic. Holy ground. I touched the indentations, formed with remarkable precision approaching something like an artist's care. I even detected what looked like a curved flourish at the end of the horizontal bar of the "T."

Had they left the parking lot yet?

Now I was running in great strides, kicking sand and, for all I knew, people as well, eager to catch up with my two fugitives. Why is that crazy man in the speedo running away from and not into the lake? I had never liked drawing attention to myself, but here I was doing exactly that. Then I stopped abruptly when I saw, about ten car-lengths away, a familiar blur of pink - Bea, standing near a station wagon, talking again to Kate and Alice.

Something Bea said a few minutes ago flew back to my ears: " . . . part of him stayed behind with me."

Dodger was sitting on his haunches, his back to me and his long tail resting on the dirt, fanning its surface. I walked forward, but just a few steps.

I yelled, the word coming instinctively from deep within, the one word I suppose I'd been longing to shout for the past three years: "Dash!"

Dodger sat still for perhaps five seconds, and when he turned to face me, his new look froze me in my tracks. Bea stooped toward him, probably because she heard him growling, something unusual for him. She still hadn't put his leash on and reached out to fasten it to his collar. The dog lunged at her, clamped his mouth to a large section of her exposed neck and wouldn't let go. His forepaws pushed her stomach, and still biting hard, he took her to ground, both of them a soundless flurry of movement and blood. Kate held Alice close and they both ran toward me, as all around us people screamed and kept their distance from the primal carnage playing out near the front wheel of the station wagon. It seemed as though the animal was trying to hide her from view by shoving her with his still biting head under the car where no one could disturb his work. A policeman, too late to be of any real help, was suddenly there, gun drawn. For a second you could see his concern that his shot might hurt the victim, but he must have quickly seen it wouldn't matter. He fired twice into the animal, and Bea's legs lay still under the dog's weight.

I wrapped Kate and Alice in my arms, but it would no doubt have been hard to tell who was comforting whom.

"Kate," I said, "come back to the beach. There's something you have to see."

Bewildered by my request as she was, part of her was no doubt glad for a chance to remove our daughter from seeing any more horror. I led them toward the rocks, past a throng of faces, many of whom were struggling to see what sort of excitement was unfolding behind us in the far section of the parking lot. Kate saw me gesturing, pointing down at the sand at the base of the rocks. We both looked down, where now there were merely random drag marks and the prints of scattered human feet.

"Daddy, what's wrong. . . what's wrong?"

Her tiny voice seemed like it was coming from a mile away. Trading one patient for another, my wife patted my cheek.

"Let's sit down, dear, until things calm down. You might be in shock. What do you mean your name was in the sand?"

Did I say that? I had no memory of saying that. She says I said that, even to this day she insists I said that.

I must have said that.

She left Alice with me for less than a minute while she ran back for our beach blanket, lying where I had left it. Then she returned, and we huddled together, bundled in a cocoon of cloth, more like refugees than vacationers, in the bright afternoon sun.

I was shivering, you see.

We listened to hushed comments from nearby groups concerning an attack of some sort back in the lot. This one had heard a gunshot, that one had heard two. Those kids over there had seen it all, that guy's wife had seen it - it was a wild dog that bit a kid - no, it was . . .

At first it sounded like a note of distant music being prolonged, but as it grew louder the closer it approached, we recognized it as a siren, no doubt from an ambulance.

"Hungry mommy."

"We'll eat a little later, honey."

"Kate, what was Bea talking about in the parking lot just before - ?"

"Nothing much, just about needing to drive over to the Mercer Dock area to pick up her husband. She said she liked my swimsuit, I complimented her on her hair. She joked about her bangs, said she only styled her hair that way to cover up her scar."

"Scar?"

"Said she fell off her bike when she was twelve, cut her head pretty bad. It was lucky her dad knew a lot of biology, so he didn't even need to take her to see a doctor. Sewed her up himself. But the scar remained. The poor thing showed it to me."

That crackling noise again, like tree branches snapping in succession, then a pause before the cries of the coasters in freefall, descending to earth, reached out to us.

My voice came out hoarse: "Well, yes Kate, they do that."

"What? They do what?"

"Scars - they remain."

THE END

HENRY JEKYLL'S GRAVESIDE SERVICE

A NOTE TO THE READER

Five years ago a box of legal documents, manuscripts and letters found their way to an office in New Scotland Yard. They originated in the estate of Jeremy Hoggles, a law professor at Oxford who had recently passed away. As it turned out, he was the great grandson of Christopher Soames, who had been, for a short time , one of the Yard's first chief inspectors of homicide in the 1880's. Somehow this material next fell into the hands of a reporter for the London Times. The end result of his involvement is the story presented here. No doubt whole sections of it will one day soon find their way into our notorious tabloid press.

That story, of course - at least part of it - has been told before, in the famous The Strange Case of Dr. Jekyll and Mr. Hyde, by Robert Louis Stevenson. Though the author almost certainly had no access to this box's contents, he clearly had heard from someone about the general events they describe. The characters who appear in his account bear fictional names of his invention, but we now know their counterparts lived and breathed over a hundred years ago in this city.

We choose to keep their identities a secret for as long as possible. Thus, you will find here the characters' names used in Mr.

Stevenson's celebrated tale. Their familiarity should create a bridge of sorts from the earlier fictional story to this one.

Chapter ONE

Though not expected at the cemetery until much later that night, he decided to observe the scheduled event here this morning as well. He stood, shrouded in London's familiar fog, while some of the mourners gathered near the main gate about fifty yards away. The number of the erect, black- clad forms increased as the sun went about its steady routine of attempting to clear the air. Knowing he was becoming as visible to them as they were to him, he began walking slowly down the sidewalk, keeping close to the stone wall that led to the closed gate.

Across the street loomed the fortress that was the Burton Hotel, and from its front doors he saw a woman and a little boy, who looked to be about ten years old, emerge and cross the street toward the throng. A dark veil covered her face, and the boy wore a rather garish green woolen cap topped off by a white puff ball of yarn. The woman held the child's hand as both joined the group.

From inside the cemetery, someone opened the gate, and both sets of the vertical black spears parted. As if on cue, two white plumes atop the heads of two black horses could be seen coming into view from around the corner of the hotel. This sight and the sound of the animals' hooves alerted the crowd to the hearse's arrival. The glass-enclosed wagon pulled up to the entrance and stopped. He watched the woman draw the boy closer to her and press a white handkerchief under her veil to wipe away a tear. The fabric's quick flutter of movement allowed him to catch a brief glimpse of what seemed a very pretty face underneath.

The undertaker and his assistant materialized and began rounding up, from the crowd, designated pallbearers who stood, two on each side, of the rear carriage wheels. He could see that the path inside the gate would not be wide enough to accommodate the hearse. Almost at once, a stately black carriage with gold plated trim around the doors pulled up behind it. He watched as the dignified form of a middle-aged gentleman got out, followed by a most familiar face to him: his own cousin, John Poole, the deceased's butler and the very reason he had become involved in this whole affair. They made eye contact and he could tell John hadn't expected to see him here this morning.

Poole made his way as unobtrusively as possible through the crowd, approached his cousin and at once conveyed his surprise at seeing him.

"I thought it best to have an early look at the territory, John, so as not to be left in the dark tonight - literally and figuratively, you could say."

"Well, as long as you've come, there's someone I'd like you to meet."

Poole led him back closer to the gate.

"Mr. Utterson, this is my cousin, Eric Latch. Eric, Mr. Utterson is - WAS Jekyll's lawyer and very good friend. Dr. Lanyon is here somewhere, too."

The pallbearers, carrying the casket, were starting toward the cobblestone path. Eric and Poole walked side by side, just behind the veiled woman and the boy.

Eric nudged his cousin and shot him an inquiring glance her way.

Poole whispered that she was Mrs. Dodge, Henry Jekyll's' sister. From behind, Eric felt a delicate tap on his shoulder, followed by a whisper in his ear.

"Now, would you be the new detective from Scotland Yard we've been hearing about?"

Eric turned to see a broad ruddy face crowned with a formidable top hat.

"I would be, sir."

"I am Hastie Lanyon, a friend and colleague of the deceased. It was Utterson's idea to invite you here later tonight. He's more concerned than I am with keeping things proper."

Utterson, close by, gave a dismissive grunt, and the woman walking next to Lanyon elbowed his ribcage.

"Oh, forgive me,dear, this is Mr. Latch - John Poole's cousin." She nodded politely at him.

"My patient, long-suffering wife, Betsy Lanyon."

Lanyon, in response to what he considered his own wit, gave himself a low chuckle.

The procession was heading a considerable distance down the path into a section of the grounds that was almost entirely vacant of tombstones. They passed a tall statue of an armored St. George on horseback, in the process of thrusting his sword into a ferocious looking dragon below. Only then did Eric realize where he was - St. George's Cemetery. Poole had only told him it was the cemetery across from the Burton Hotel, and Eric had been a stranger to it until now.

Eventually they left the path, crossed a patch of grass and stopped at a newly dug grave just a little ways from a monument to a family named Turner. Over that adjacent grave hovered a nearly life-sized sculpted angel with a fittingly sad face. While the other mourners gathered round the casket and the undertaker placed a large bouquet of lilacs on its lid, Eric thought he'd approach Jekyll's sister. He walked the short distance to her and bowed his head.

"May I offer my sympathy on the loss of your brother,Madam. I was very briefly a patient of his, and he was very kind to me."

"He was always very kind to everyone. His nephew and I shall miss him. And your name is?"

"Eric Latch."

He returned to stand next to Poole, his heart pounding.

The church itself, St. George's, stood not far away, behind a picket fence, but the vicarage had, for some strange reason, been built across from the church on the other side of Pierce Street. The bell from the steeple began tolling, slowly, eight times. Several of the gentlemen round the grave instinctively looked at their pocket watches, impatient for the minister's arrival.

***

As the eighth bell reverberated across the neighborhood, the front door of the vicarage opened, and the Reverend Charles Trancer crossed the street to the walkway that led along the side of the church to the fence. Nearly all of the mourners watched his approach.

The cleric still hadn't reconciled himself to the disappointing breakfast his wife had just laid before him: two buttered biscuits, coffee and a bowl of oatmeal. Where were the fried eggs, rashers, tomatoes and toast that were his due every day? Her excuse of not feeling well was specious at best and at worst defiant. What would be the outcome, he wondered, were he to shirk his duty as she neglected hers?

He noticed now a surprisingly sizable number of mourners waiting. The vicar knew that one of them undoubtedly must be Lawyer Utterson, one of the finest legal minds in the city. One of his young clerks had paid Reverend Trancer a visit two days ago to make arrangements for this doctor's interment in the recently acquired cemetery property. Upon agreeing to this proposal, the vicar had been handed a personal check for one hundred pounds as a donation to the church.

He scanned the crowd for familiar faces but found none. They all resembled professional types, some of them no doubt professors from the medical college the deceased had once attended; some of his fellow physicians, surely - oh, and there were a few women - could be they were nurses from that free clinic this Doctor Jackson - Jackridge- whatever ridiculous name it was - had opened in White Chapel, for the poor. The veiled woman - who was she? He hadn't thought the deceased was married . . . and that idiotic hat on that young brat next to her! So much anxiety to deal with already today, and the morning had barely begun.

He had forgotten to put on his surplice which was folded over his arm. Taking his place at the head of the grave, he made a great show of waving the garment in the breeze and drawing its opening down over his shiny bald head.

Clutching his black leather prayer book to his chest, he stared around at the somber faces and hoped his face wore an expression of at least some sympathy, though this was a talent that he had often struggled to master but seldom achieved. He then gazed heavenward, hoping for the best.

When he began to speak, his voice was suitably rich but devoid of genuine feeling, as if knowing Jekyll had hardly ever entered his church and no doubt had, as a scientist, nothing but disdain for the faith. Why, he wondered, do such people or their families bother to insist on rituals such as these? None the less, the familiar scriptural phrases of hope and comfort tumbled effortlessly from his pious mouth. When he finished, he saw the veiled woman give her son, still wearing the strange green hat, an envelope which quickly found its way into his extended palm.

"My mother and I thank you for your kind words, sir."

Young Detective Latch then observed Dr.Lanyon bend and whisper a few words to his wife. She appeared anxious as he left her to approach the gravedigger who stood nearby under an elm, hunched over a shovel. The doctor spoke a few words to him and dropped some coins into the man's hand. As Lanyon returned to his wife, Eric watched the gravedigger begin walking back toward the caretaker's lodge near the front gate.

Lanyon, Utterson, Jekyll's sister and her son were making hushed plans to attend a simple, intimate breakfast in one of the Burton Hotel's private dining rooms across the street .

Latch thought it might be a good time to nonchalantly follow the gravedigger, whose name he knew to be Billy, and leave the others to go on their way. By the time he reached the lodge, his quarry was coming back out, shouldering a large rolled carpet, no shovel to be seen.

"Odd to see you without your shovel, Billy."

Gazing up with a wary eye, he instantly turned friendly when he recognized the familiar face of one of the many young coppers recently hired by the yard.

Billy himself was a peculiar looking fellow, all told. Short in stature with the zest and agility of a youngster, yet he had the face and hairline of an old man. An extremely high forehead gave way to no more than a few tufts of the palest blond hair. And you didn't have to look very closely to notice lines on his forehead and cheeks that lent him a wizened character. He would often like to tell his pals that even as a child his mum often laughingly referred to him as her "little old man."

"The fellow in charge of the party," Billy began, "doesn't want the casket covered with dirt until just after midnight. Very irregular, most unusual. But mind you sir, I'm not complaining. He's paid me handsomely for the inconvenience.'

"Still," said Latch, "it is odd, isn't it?"

"Said something about the family holding to odd superstitions, sir. Might be they're Scotch or Irish."

"Most likely, Billy" replied the detective agreeably, yet inwardly cringing on behalf of his dear relatives in Dublin.

A gravedigger who would have to wait until tonight to do his work under a midnight moon. . . what sort of mystery had Eric stumbled into, anyway?

****

147

Chapter TWO

It had begun just the day before with a surprising visit at the Yard from his cousin, John Poole. Both of their mothers were sisters, and the boys had been raised in the same household through childhood and most of their formative years. Yet their contacts during the last fifteen years or so were few, as each had pursued different tracks: Eric's took him to a few years in her majesty's army in India and now this post in the Yard; Poole's track had taken him toward some schooling and years of service as a butler to a prominent physician here in the city. So both had been drawn to London, quite far from their home village of Glenford on the outskirts of Dublin.

Viewed in ordinary tweeds and street attire, Poole displayed little of the stark formality conveyed by his butler's uniform. Physically fit and well put together, he had the overall bearing of a strong laborer or soldier.

"Cousin John, what a wonderful surprise!"

"Look at you, your very own office here already!"

"Not quite. It's merely a room we're allowed to use to do our paper work or conduct interviews. The other fellows are all out and about, so we should be able to chat here for a bit."

Eric saw a cloud quickly darken John's face.

"Here, what's wrong old man?"

Poole sat down at the work table across from his cousin, unbuttoning his shirt collar and shifting uncomfortably in the chair.

"I'm afraid this isn't just a social call, Eric. Things have been very distressing lately - all having to do with my- uh- my master. You met him, I recall, at the house once."

"Yes. You recommended I see him for a check-up regarding my war injury. A charming fellow, did me a world of good. And you've been with him for some time?"

"Twelve years."

Poole abruptly lowered his head and addressed his next words directly to the floor.

"He's dead, died just a few days ago. We're burying him tomorrow."

"Good god, what was the cause? He seemed the picture of health when I saw him."

"It was not long after your visit that he began to take a downward turn. Frankly, I don't know where to begin, Eric."

"His name was . . . what was it now?"

Poole showed a flash of annoyance.

"Jekyll- Henry Jekyll."

"Of course. I'm sorry - a distinctive name. So you'll be seeking employment elsewhere."

Poole stood up quickly and went to the window, his back to his cousin,and began talking instead to the sheets of rain that were hitting the glass.

"There's so much you don't know, Eric - so much. But to put your mind at ease lest you're worried about how I"m to earn my living- I've just come from Henry's- Dr. Jekyll's- lawyer. He confirmed what I've already known for years . . . I'm to receive a substantial bequest in his will. So you needn't fret that I've come here for a hand-out."

"You may be sure no such worry crossed my -"

"Forgive my outburst - it's just that I need a moment to collect myself."

Nothing but silence from behind him at the window. Then, awkwardly, a heavy sigh that sounded almost like a gasp caused Eric to turn to see him sobbing, head bowed, inconsolable. Instinctively he was at his relative's side, guiding him back to the chair. In a few seconds he'd removed two glasses from a cabinet and poured whiskey for both of them. Now they were sitting, facing each other once more.

"Is there anything I can do for you, John? Please tell me exactly why you're here, and I'll do all I can to -"

"It was Utterson, Henry's lawyer, who brought up your name, Eric. I hadn't even thought of you regarding this matter. It turns out that Henry once mentioned to Utterson that you'd just been hired at Scotland Yard. No doubt I'd been bragging about you to Henry - regarding your new position. So here I sit, asking for your assistance. It's Utterson, you see, who wants a police presence to witness what we plan to do in the cemetery tomorrow night. Since you're my blood relative, we thought we might count on your sympathy - "

Puzzled, Eric struggled to keep exasperation out of the tone of his reply.

"You yourself say there's a great deal I don't know, but you're doing nothing but confusing me. Surely you're not planning to bury him at night! "

"Of course not, the funeral will be tomorrow at eight a.m., but we plan to return to the grave again after sunset."

Eric watched as Poole resorted to an old nervous childhood habit. He shaded his eyes with one hand, tilted his head down a bit and began tapping the fingers of his other hand slowly, rhythmically on the table. Only after giving his cousin enough time to calm down did Eric make an attempt to forge ahead.

"Alright, John, you lost your employer - to whom you were devoted as one would be to a friend. That much I understand."

"He was more than my employer and even more than a friend, I'm afraid."

"Oh, I know how common it is for servants and masters to form strong ties of mutual dependence. But what I don't understand is -"

Now it was Poole whose exasperation surfaced.

"You don't understand the first thing about anything, lad. I hope you're better at putting together clues in your crime-solvings than you are here with me. Henry Jekyll and I first met fourteen years ago here in the city at St. Luke's medical school as students. We've been together ever since- intimately- yes, as lovers. We cooked up the deception of me posing as his butler only as an excuse for us living together. It began almost as a kind of joke, but really I soon began to enjoy the charade, sort of like playing a part on the stage."

On at least two occasions during Poole's confession, Eric would put his finger to his lips, walk to the closed door and open it to check the foot traffic in the hall. He would then tiptoe quickly back to his chair to continue listening to his cousin's story.

"As far as the maid, the cook or visitors were concerned, and needless to say the patients, I was the doctor's butler. Both servants arrived in the morning and left at six. I stayed, Henry's live-in butler. Our bedrooms were separated by an adjoining door. Pour yourself another drink, Eric. This tale is just getting started."

"I'd completely forgotten you were in medical training for a bit. But do be careful, John,
as to whom you confess such revelations. You should need no reminder that - -"

"Oh, damn it all! I know I could be sent to prison! Well, I suppose I've come to the right place then to unburden myself today. Yes, Henry and I were in St. Luke's together taking classes, but we hardly knew each other for the longest time. I was two years ahead of him, nearly ready to graduate with a degree, when another young man and I were caught in a back room of the library . . . let's just say in a compromising position. We were both expelled - though grateful to the dean for not having us arrested. Eric, I had so hoped no one in our family would ever hear about this wretched business."

Eric assured him that no one, least of all anyone else in their family, would ever hear a word of this from him.

"Anyway, Henry got wind of this messy business and came to my dormitory room on
the very day I was packing to move out. He expressed sympathy - I thought at great risk to himself. I could instantly see we had things in common - if you know what I mean. That is how our relationship

began, Eric. I managed to get by for a couple of years getting odd jobs here and there. For a while I was a bartender at a pub just around the corner from this very building. I noted it as I came in."

"The King's Carrot? You worked there?"

"For nearly a year, until Henry graduated and began to set up his private practice. It was in that very establishment where we first planned our elaborate - well I suppose one must call it a deception, mustn't one?"

Eric was trying as much as possible to exhibit a relaxed demeanor, despite his genuine astonishment at this view into his cousin's forbidden private life. He was surprised at how easily he was able to convey the warmth and understanding John seemed to need so desperately.

"I'm sure you and your doctor were not the only bachelors to have had to resort to such subterfuge in order to be together."

"You don't know what it means - finally to be able to speak openly about this to you, Eric. Even as children I longed to broach the subject to you."

The young detective extended his hand across the table, giving his cousin's arm a firm clasp.

"But I'm correct in assuming that you came here to discuss more than these matters, have you not?"

"Indeed, Eric. These "matters" as you call them now seem merely a light-hearted prologue to the horrors I've witnessed these last few months. . ."

"You won't mind, John, if I take some notes while you tell me all about it?"

He seemed alarmed, but only briefly.

"I suppose it can do no harm . . . since poor Henry's gone now."

Two hours later the bottle of whiskey was empty, John Poole had just closed the door behind him on his way out, and Detective Latch sat staring open-mouthed at the rain beyond the window as it continued to fall like a heavy curtain all over London.

****

Chapter THREE

If John had not, in the interview, referred to a criminal matter - and not just ANY criminal matter, but the notorious murder of Sir Danvers Carew, Eric would have probably been content to go about his regular duties at the Yard that day. But from the moment Poole left, the entire business weighed heavily on him. He asked one of the clerks to tell Chief Inspector Soames he was ill, grabbed some writing supplies and dashed off to his rooms at Mrs. Neff's.

It was there he spent the rest of the afternoon and early evening transcribing a somewhat official report of the strange interview he'd conducted that day. Reluctant, at least for the time being, to divulge the subject's name, he referred to him as precisely just that: the subject. If Eric were to witness anything tomorrow evening in the cemetery that could be construed as harmful or illegal, he would then submit the report to Chief Soames, along with his reasons for delaying to take immediate action.

He would have to trust his own judgment in this matter and hope that the common sense of Dr. Jekyll's two friends would prevail. Lawyer Utterson and Dr. Lanyon were gentlemen, it seemed, who were held in high esteem in London society.

Eric would naturally write nothing of his cousin's distasteful confession concerning his relationship with his employer. Jekyll's death, fortunately, had at least put an end to all that.

What follows, then, are the contents of that report, as placed in an envelope and sealed by Eric Latch just after midnight; a report that approximately twenty-four hours later he would either hand over to his superior or destroy. He eagerly hoped it would be the latter.

***   ***   ***

The subject began by saying that thirteen years ago young Dr. Jekyll was able to afford to purchase the house on the fashionable Trent Square due to a large inheritance from his father. Laurence Jekyll, an Edinburgh banker, died not long before the doctor took his degree from St. Luke's Medical School. Henry's older sister Susan also received a substantial bequest, but was herself married by this time and residing in London. Within months of his graduation, he began to develop a thriving practice as word spread about both his skill and pleasing ways. He strove to nurture his commitment to social reform by soliciting funds to open a much needed free clinic for the poor in White Chapel. Indeed the subject claimed the doctor spent more time tending to the wretches there than he did at his home office, where his patients were mostly people of breeding.

Any extra time he had was devoted to the experiments and research he conducted in his private study and laboratory in the cellar of his house, a large space which he had specially converted soon after taking up residence. According to the subject, these experiments had their origin in Jekyll's deeply held belief that each of us harbors within ourselves a darker nature, only released or apparent during times of stress or passion.

Extremely intent in pursuing this theory toward an outcome, he was trying to create a way for this alter ego to become physically visible for long periods of time .He claimed a transformation could be possible not only in a man's personality but also in his biological make-up and physiognomy, thereby creating a new identity separate from his original self. Henry hoped this would eventually come to pass by means of the combination of certain powders and salts that would form a potion, an elixir that would initiate the process.

The subject went on to say that he had on many occasions witnessed the delivery of countless cages, boxes and containers to the house's rear cellar entrance - many of which held small animals needed for the experiments .

Henry would occasionally go out for dinner with friends or invite colleagues to dine with him. Now and then the conversation would turn to Jekyll's theory and research, but as he became more determined and passionate in expressing himself to his guests, he was too often met with derision. He and his colleagues would have by this time left the ladies in the dining room and retired to the parlor for their cherished privacy.

There, free from the constraints of propriety and good manners, several of them, on more than one occasion, accused Jekyll of blasphemy. It was especially disheartening for him one night when Dr. Lanyon, his dearest friend, bellowed in a rage no doubt heard in the street.

"Continue along this path, Henry, and the only clinic you'll be running will be from your very own cell in Broadmoor!"

Crushed by such ridicule from his peers, Henry retreated for long periods of time from society, choosing instead to devote larger amounts of time to his experiments.

One afternoon in March, just four months ago, Henry Jekyll, looking both haggard and euphoric, approached the subject with news of "the greatest breakthrough." His darker self, kept prisoner in the depths of his soul, had finally seen the light of day. The subject recalls asking, a bit facetiously no doubt, just where this nasty man might be. Henry tapped his chest, winking playfully.

"Back in the box," he replied and then added, "for the time being."

The subject, sensing the doctor was eager to show off his achievement, agreed to come to the laboratory later that night. Once there, he watched Jekyll pour a brownish liquid from a beaker into a small glass and swallow the contents. For a while it seemed as though nothing was going to happen. Then the doctor wiped his brow with a cloth and gripped the edge of the lab table with both hands as if waiting for an onslaught to commence.

The first effects were strangely subtle: beads of perspiration on the face and neck, a new paleness to the complexion and an odd prominence to veins on the forehead and throat. Suddenly a hoarse gasping for breath issued from his mouth, along with a bending and twisting of the shoulders. The mouth, as if pulled from within, yawned in a painful grimace revealing a grotesque enlargement of teeth; the hair, always Henry's crown of golden curls, now began to flatten, lengthening into a dark, greasy mat that nearly covered his eyes.

The eyes were most difficult for the subject to behold. Once twin lights of tenderness and easy charm, they glared now like orbs of ink, pools of dark malice. Muscular contractions were now apparent under Jekyll's shirt and trousers, causing him to bite the back of his hand to stifle cries of anguish. He would later describe the pain as probably equal to a woman's during childbirth; though certainly worse, due to its being located over every inch of his frame. Most unusual of all, though, was the shrinking of Henry's stature to the height of a very short man, along with the widening of his upper torso., Finally he arched his body backward as a long violent shudder coursed through his extremities, causing him to collapse onto the floor.

For at least two or three minutes the subject was certain the doctor was dead and worried about how he would explain to authorities the presence of this monster-like corpse in the house. Then he watched in amazement as the rumpled shape behind the table stirred, in clothes that were now almost comically too big, and lift himself up from the floor. The creature looked as startled to see the subject as the subject was to see him.

"Who are you?" asked the creature, its voice rough and parched.

The subject identified himself, and the creature, puzzled, stroked the coarse stubble on its cheek and nodded its head.

"Ah yes, I'm beginning to recall things - though it's not easy, you know."

The creature moved closer, extended his short, hairy, unfamiliar fingers and reached up to grab the subject's shoulders.

"We have to work on getting me a new wardrobe, don't we?"

The subject attempted to absorb the full extent of the horror he was staring at, inches away. (Indeed at such moments the subject's description of these fantastic events was so powerful that they seemed to have sprung to life here in our detectives' workroom at the Yard).The subject went on: The creature's foul odor and breath began to overpower him and nearly cause him to faint. The last thing he can remember the creature saying was:

"New clothes,yes! Mustn't be seen around this town unless I'm looking my best!"

So it was that the subject lent his assistance in the ensuing days to providing Henry Jekyll with a new flat of rooms in a less fashionable part of the city. This location would allow Edward Hyde, for that was the name Jekyll gave him, a place to call home during the hours, mostly nights, when he planned to lead his life of debauchery - free from the scruples and morality of the good doctor.

It was Jekyll himself who personally had a talk with his cook and housekeeper regarding the occasional comings and goings of his "new friend," Mr. Hyde, who was to have unlimited access to the house at any time; he indicated to both of them that Poole, the butler, had also been apprised of the new situation, and that no one was to question this stranger's presence in the house- even if he should be occasionally glimpsed upstairs . The doctor described Hyde to them as suffering from a muscular deformity, particularly of the face, adding that the gentleman would always behave politely toward them and would just prefer not to be engaged in any conversation whenever they might encounter him.

The subject recalled one particular morning when Henry revealed that just the night before he had paid a call on Hastie Lanyon, whom he had not seen since the flare-up at the dinner party. Lanyon was surprised not only to see his friend, but to note that he arrived carrying his black bag. It contained, of course, the potion - and in ten minutes or so Betsy Lanyon, upstairs, heard her husband cry out from below. In a flurry of panic she ran downstairs to the dining room, where she saw her husband, standing with his mouth agape and his face a frosty white. On the floor, its back to her, a strange, bulky form was reaching for a glass that had apparently fallen. The man shoved it into a leather bag and, getting up, kept his head down and pushed rudely past her as he darted quickly toward the front door.

The subject even more vividly recollected an incident nearly a week later when the morning newspaper arrived with a headline story regarding the murder of Sir Danvers Carew the night before. This was a man known to Jekyll as one of the chief donors of his White Chapel clinic for the poor. Jekyll visibly trembled as he read the account, then finally slapped the paper down next to his breakfast plate with a flourish.

"Balderdash!" he cried, "They claim they're at a loss to imagine a motive for anyone wanting to bash the kindly old gentleman's head in! I'll give them a motive!"

The doctor rose from his table, went to the window and after a half minute passed during which he calmed down, continued.

"No doubt the assailant saw in Carew's refined and oh, so civilized demeanor the very type of warm-hearted old fellow Henry Jekyll would eventually grow to be in his old age. Well, my good friend Hyde simply could not abide that notion. It was that very idea I feel certain fueled his killer instinct and caused him to strike out with his cane . . . so savagely. "

The subject specifically remembers Jekyll uttering the last two words in a whisper of bitterness and shame. Jekyll turned to face his confidante.

"You're saying it was you, Henry?"

"Not I." There was an odd hoarseness in his voice. "It was Hyde."

Only a few days later Henry, dishevelled and anxious, sought the subject out yet again to share another terror. On the preceding night while strolling through Crawford Park on his way to meet Utterson at their club for drinks, he felt a slight dizziness that caused him to sit on a bench. He sat in the grip of abject horror as the unmistakable tremors of the familiar seizures began to vibrate under his flesh. Arms, legs, shoulders and neck - all quivered with the new approaching life. Obviously the transformation was now able to occur without the ingestion of the drug! Bewildered but quickly accepting the unannounced visit from his friend, he realized he could no longer meet his lawyer. Instead he decided to walk toward his new digs in Soho and whatever delightful amusements might await him there.

The subject then began to speak of the tragedy that had occurred just three nights before his interview with me. He was made aware of Jekyll's intention to take his own life. Desperate to prevent this, he ran to Trent Square where he shoved his shoulders repeatedly into the locked door of the doctor's bedroom. A syringe, drained of its lethal contents, lay on the sheet next to the bare arm of Henry Jekyll. The subject claims to have instinctively cast his eyes around the room, expecting to see "the other one" crouching somewhere in the shadows. But there was, of course, only Henry, lying motionless and cold on the bed.

Next came a story of a transformation that was perhaps equally as shocking as the previous ones recounted here. Lawyer Utterson and Dr. Lanyon were sent for and, after viewing Jekyll's body, made their way down to the laboratory, where, in plain sight, on the top of one of the tables rested the journal in which Jekyll had recorded all of his experiments. Lanyon seemed especially enthralled by it for hours afterward, while Utterson merely fussed about how he was going to avoid involving the police in the ugly business. With influential friends such as these, the subject felt Jekyll's reputation would doubtless remain unblemished. Just after sending a street urchin for the undertaker, Lanyon poured some of Henry's finest bourbon and all three made themselves comfortable in the parlour.

By this time they had become aware of Jekyll's success - if such a word can be applied to his work. Lanyon had witnessed one of the transformations himself a few weeks before and spoken of it the very next morning to Utterson. The subject now told them what he knew of the murder of Danvers Carew. Horrified, Lanyon poured another bourbon, placed the journal on a table next to them and tapped his fingers on the leather cover.

"Terrible, terrible business no doubt of it," he murmured. "Though there might still be a way to make some good of it all."

The subject and Utterson exchanged questioning glances.

"Jekyll," he continued, "was not only an excellent student- he was also a very good teacher"

Employing a professorial classroom gesture, he picked up the journal with an easy familiarity.

"I am determined to duplicate this potion, gentlemen!"

The question was: why would anyone want to do such a thing? And it was the subject himself who posed it, noticing a new glint of fire in Lanyon's eyes that made him fearful. He recalled Jekyll's own bright enthusiasm when first beginning his endeavors months earlier.

"I am certain," the doctor continued, "that by making some adjustments- refinements shall we say, to Henry's formula, that I can significantly alter and improve the outcome of his work."

Utterson, growing increasingly restless and vexed, pointed an accusatory finger at his friend.

"From the very first, Lanyon, you've opposed Jekyll in his research - and now you do such a turnabout! What in god's name has gotten into you?"

The subject also claims to have voiced his own bewilderment as well.

"Surely," he said, "you cannot intend to drink the filthy brew yourself?"

"Indeed I do not," and there followed a pause that can only be described as dramatic, before he added, "I will inject the new serum into the lifeless body of our dear friend Henry, thus restoring him to us -whole and intact -as we've known him for lo these many years."

Utterson, enraged now, recalled Lanyon's own charge of blasphemy that he had leveled against Jekyll just weeks before.

"And now you yourself plan to raise the dead!"

Lanyon's response was frightening in its logic.

"Henry died of no external wound, no bullet or dagger's blade invaded his body, nor was he bludgeoned or strangled. He met no violent end. He drifted off, gentlemen, under the influence of a heavy dose of morphine. There is no reason why a new chemical substance, modeled after his own potion, might not revive him."

"Well," said the lawyer, "when you put it like that . . ."

But Utterson remained clearly worried and unconvinced.

The subject couldn't help but wonder if he was privy to the conversation of learned men or if it was perhaps the bourbon now that was doing the talking.

Soon the undertaker arrived, and Utterson instructed him to take the casket back to the cellar entrance and down to the laboratory. By this time the three men had already carried Jekyll down and were in the process of undressing their friend, sponging him off with warm water and soap. Arrangements were made to have a large shipment of ice delivered to preserve the corpse, the undertaker having been ordered to forego any embalming procedures and not even allowed to sew the doctor's lips shut. While re-dressing their friend in his finest dark suit, they noted the healthy texture and form of Henry's body, as well as the total absence of any trace of Edward Hyde lurking beneath his skin.

Jekyll's only relatives, a married sister named Susan Dodge and her son, were notified that the funeral would be on Thursday morning in St. George's Cemetery. Since they lived on the outskirts of the city, Utterson made arrangements for them to spend a few nights at the Burton Hotel directly across the street from the churchyard.

For the next twenty-four hours, with Jekyll's own corpse on ice in the open casket on the laboratory floor, Dr. Lanyon, with the assistance of the subject, worked tirelessly re-assembling the chemicals and powders he hoped would re-animate his friend. He, Utterson, and the subject planned to return to the cemetery on Thursday evening. They made plans to instruct the caretaker just prior to the morning service not to cover the grave until after midnight. That would assuredly give Lanyon more than enough time to descend into the open grave and inject the new serum into Jekyll's arm. All three would then keep a vigil over the grave and await the result.

But Lawyer Utterson continued to be troubled. Shouldn't someone from the police, someone they knew or trusted, be notified or even be present on the scene? If passersby were to witness their activity in the churchyard after dark, mightn't the whole situation be interpreted as grave robbing - especially with Doctor Lanyon there? Newspapers had been buzzing for years about the lengths to which surgeons might resort to supply cadavers for their students to dissect. Besides, Utterson added, if the intended miracle did occur and Jekyll did revive, it would be an astounding news event. Surely all London would be shocked and amazed, would want to know all the facts. It would be beneficial to have a policeman for Utterson to work with, preferably someone who could be induced to turn a blind eye toward charges of tampering with a corpse. And, which was even more likely, what if, instead of Jekyll reviving, it was Hyde who hopped out of the grave? Wouldn't it be best to have a copper there to help subdue the fiend and bring the killer of Danvers Carew to justice?

All of Utterson's worries, according to the subject, made Lanyon uneasy, consumed as he was with ideas of the fame and great personal achievement that now seemed within his grasp. The subject and Lanyon were clearly dismayed by the lawyer's anxieties, and succeeded in calming him only when the subject claimed he knew one of the new inspectors at Scotland Yard and would seek his discreet assistance sometime before the day of the funeral.

The end result of this debate was that the subject approached me this morning to tell me ever so much more than he'd been instructed to reveal. Utterson and Lanyon had asked him only to request my presence tomorrow night at St. George's Cemetery in case "anything unusual" should occur. I consider all three gentlemen respectable professionals merely attempting, astounding as it is to say, to bring their dear friend back to life.

The subject ended the interview by suggesting it might be wise for me to bring along a gun, adding that he was very much eager to see me at the cemetery across from the Burton Hotel tomorrow night, near Jekyll's grave.
report.

************ *************

Chapter FOUR

Across the Thames the sun lowers into a cloud, but before disappearing sends a rich orange glow across the cemetery. Eric gives an approving nod on the entire scene and strikes a match, re-lighting the tobacco in the bowl of his pipe. He is sitting on a ledge of stone that surrounds the base of a monument to a family named Hudson, of which two sisters rest - he hopes - comfortably under his feet. Jekyll's grave lies about a hundred yards away across a bare expanse of grass, at the base of a hill, a grove of bushes and trees just behind it, separating it from the vicar's gate.

He hadn't thought much about the grave's secluded location this morning at the funeral service, but now assumes this was planned by Lanyon and the lawyer to give them the privacy their little adventure tonight might require. A solitary stone, rather distinct, stands adjacent to the doctor's open grave and is just now catching the fire of the sunset. About three feet off the ground, the surface of the marble supports a heroically carved angel, wings extending up from his shoulders. He is stooping and extending both arms downward, seeming to suggest grief or possibly a tribute to whatever souls lie under his watch.

Eric occasionally visits the British museum and is rather fond of sculpture. It would be a perfect place to take Maureen. . . Maureen - he tries to recall the last name of the cheerful new girl at Garland's Florist shop. Perhaps he'll work up the courage to ask. . . ah, he feels a sharp cool change in the air now. Bracing, it makes him focus for a while on whatever duties might be expected of him tonight.

His mind wanders again , though, to thoughts of how he'll phrase his offer of taking Maureen to the museum and how jolly it might be to hold her hand strolling from exhibit to exhibit. But for some reason Poole pops into his mind. How could a bloke feel that way about another bloke anyway? Serving his time in India and familiar these days with all sorts of criminal types abroad here in the city, Eric senses there probably is more of that business going on than most people might think. Yet he hates to picture John in that way and, for that matter, even Dr. Jekyll himself whom he met that one time. They both seemed such ordinary chaps that afternoon, showing no signs of being sissies or nancy boys. Both presented themselves as rather stalwart, sturdy fellows - even the doctor appearing he could hold his own as an athlete or even in a brawl if he had to. Summers -that was her name, Maureen Summers - lovely girl.

Twilight has been quick to plant deeper shadows that now lie all across the graveyard, the angel having become a vague gray lump; but darker than everything out there on the ground is the black rectangle of Jekyll's open grave. Eric taps his pipe empty on the edge of his stony seat and realizes he has spent more time today among the dead than ever before in his life. Better get used to it, he thinks, his own time will come soon enough. He remembers, too, so many of his mates who never made it back from India.

The low un-birdlike moan of an owl, doubtless in one of the trees beyond the grave, disturbs the quiet. He feels the bulky weight of the gun in the large inside pocket of his coat, a derringer won in a poker game in Calcutta. He decided not to requisition one from the Yard earlier, since his time here tonight could not rightly be called official business. When he showed his weapon to his uncle last year, the old man had jokingly commented that it looked like a toy pirate pistol. Still, Eric feels confident it'll serve its purpose, even on the remote chance he'd need it in this dismal place.

A rush of movement behind him brings him to his feet. It is Utterson, wearing a mischievous grin that looks forced and not quite genuine.

"Just seeing you, Detective, sends all my worries packing."

"If you're so worried, sir, why didn't you stay home?"

"Friendship," says the lawyer, "makes a man do strange things."

Eric asks where Poole and Lanyon are. Utterson replies they're coming together in the latter's carriage. He himself has just come from dining in the hotel with Henry's sister Susan and her boy who will be returning home tomorrow.

A detail troubles Eric.

"How did you gain entrance to the cemetery? Wasn't the main gate locked?"

"I have a key. Now don't you trouble yourself about how I managed that. I might just as easily pose the same question to you, Mr. Latch."

Eric, just as quick with his response, replied that he had used the vicar's gate in the fence he had noticed this morning. But now he senses a more serious expression and tone of voice creeping over the lawyer.

"I was talking to your chief at the yard about what my two friends are intending to do here tonight."

Eric steps back, astonished.

"I say! You'll be getting me sacked, sir."

"No indeed - you needn't worry there."

Utterson stoops, places a large hand on his shoulder and gently guides the younger man toward the cobblestone path and a bench on which they sit.

Clearly the lawyer has a great deal to say.

"Yes, I heard your relative paid you a call yesterday. Mostly that was due to my urging. Chief Inspector Soames is a great friend of mine, so you needn't fear getting into any hot water over any of this. What I'm most vexed about, you see, is my professional reputation. As Henry's lawyer and nearly lifelong friend, I have been privy to all sorts of conversations with him over the years - matters related to his income, his estate, his will and even some personal relationships. Although Henry never married, still there are questionable things, you know. Lately there's been this rumor involving a potion or drug he may have invented, and now Lanyon and even your cousin Poole wanting to come to this godforsaken place to violate his corpse - and suicide itself, you know, is always such a frightful mess."

Utterson is clearly beside himself with agitation. High above, a passing cloud uncovers a nearly full moon, its pale light revealing a wild look in his eyes. He pulls a flask from a pocket, proffering it first to Eric who refuses politely.

"There's something wrong with both of them, you see. I'm convinced of it. But especially Lanyon - I think he's become unstable- mentally, I'm quite certain of it. There's even talk that

Jekyll might have done a murder, or at least knew who is responsible. It's as though I'm surrounded by criminals or crazy people, Mr. Latch. You must be my rock tonight!"

"I'll do my best, Mr. Utterson."

They get up and walk along the path in the direction of the front gate, but after taking only a few steps, Utterson stops and grabs both of Eric's shoulders.

"That conversation you had with Poole yesterday - how did it go?"

Eric seems uneasy at the directness of the inquiry.

"Really, sir, much of what he said was in the strictest confidence."

"Oh, I know you're cousins and all that, but - "

"It's not just that. I do feel an obligation to the Yard. Even though I may be one of the newer detectives, there is something vaguely disturbing about your requesting my being here tonight. And since you've already referred to a murder, we must be talking about the Carew affair. Solving that case is a top priority with my superiors, you see."

The lawyer is becoming more impatient by the minute.

"May I at least ask you how long the two of you spoke about these matters?"

"I would say nearly two and a half hours, sir."

Apoplectic is not too extreme an adjective to describe Utterson's reaction.

"Good lord, man, he was only supposed to ask you to come here in an unofficial capacity - one simple question!"

"It could be he got carried away since we hadn't the chance to talk for a while - and I was taking notes as well."

"Look, Mr. Latch, whatever he may have told you may perhaps be tinted with his own prejudices, so I would caution you to - "

"Prejudices," he interrupts, "I don't understand."

"He has also shared some things with Lanyon and me these past two days. Did you know, for example, that Poole has always envied you?"

"Envied me!"

It is now Eric's turn to be shocked.

166

"Your heroic deeds in India did earn you a medal, and the ease with which you were hired by the Yard was yet another feather in your cap. I think he always felt inferior to you. Poole, you must remember , was expelled from medical college and has been, at least nominally, a servant for the past twelve years. I find him to be a man eager to impress others with his importance."

The detective is stunned to hear these remarks.

"But he has never given me any indication he harbors - "

"Ah, there you have it, my good fellow. He is an expert at hiding his true feelings. Sometimes I think even Henry never really knew him, despite . . ."

The sound of a horse drawn carriage's approach can be heard pulling up near the fence.

"Mr. Utterson," Latch whispers, "best wait here. No need to attract too much attention to ourselves, is there?"

"Right you are, good thinking."

And then mumbling close to Latch's ear, "I've instructed Soames to assign a couple of extra bobbies around the perimeter of this place, but they wont be here for a while. I don't know, I don't know. I have such strange fears. Well, we should look on this as humoring Lanyon - there's not a chance in heaven a dead man will walk tonight. I don't think even Poole believes it, though he did assist Lanyon with creating this new drug."

So they wait on the path, watching as Lanyon and Poole get out of the carriage, leaving the driver to wait up front. The music of a small orchestra playing a waltz somewhere in the hotel across the way lends what to Eric seems an incongruous touch to the whole affair. The two new arrivals remain on the sidewalk, bent over, engaged in some activity for a short time. Now they straighten up, both carrying lit lanterns, and head for the gate.

Eric tries valiantly, but with little success, to shake Utterson's comments about Poole from his thoughts.

"Good, we're all here!" shouts Lanyon , their swaying lamplights revealing the two shadowy figures ahead. Utterson reminds him to speak softly, that they're not in Piccadilly. Latch sees what the doctor carries in his other hand: his small black bag, surely containing the solution and syringe he'll soon need. Poole also carries something in his other hand, a rather long, intricately carved wooden cane, a support he hadn't needed this morning at the service. It could be of some use as a weapon, the detective thinks.

A wind comes up as the four leave the path and cross over to the grassy downslope toward Jekyll's grave. It waits for them like a hole in their lives, Latch is thinking. Is he turning into a poet? He can't help but consider, despite the palpable tension in the air, the great affection these men must harbor for the deceased - to risk exposing themselves in such a foolish, risky attempt to bring him back to the world of the living. Surely, what they are about to attempt will yield nothing but disappointment. Even supposing Jekyll had undergone some grotesque transformation while under the influence of his potion. . . that was indeed a far cry from inventing a drug that could bring life back to a corpse dead now for four days.

He stands a few feet from the grave and observes the three gentlemen just ahead of him standing at the pit's very edge, gazing down in silence. Eric feels like a stage hand waiting in the wings for a dark dramatic scene to be performed, by actors who have carefully rehearsed their gestures and words. He, however, is the only spectator - he and the mournful, bereft ,granite angel crouching just over there in the lamplight's glow.

********** **********

Chapter FIVE

Poole removes his long dark coat and, like the experienced manservant he is, folds it carefully, placing it on the ground. His white shirt creates a ghostly presence as, holding his cane, he gets down and crawls the few inches to the grave's edge.

"Lanyon, hold your lantern lower! I hope your undertaker didn't forget our instructions not to nail the damn thing shut." He thrusts his cane down and with both arms puts pressure on the lid.

They hear the welcome sound of wood scraping on wood and gaze down in awe. Henry's still handsome face in repose is lit from above by Lanyon's trembling lantern and, much higher still, the moon. With considerable dexterity, Poole twists the cane and manages to place its crook under the lid's rim, flipping the entire wooden cover with an audible thud against the wall of dirt on the opposite side. He lifts himself into a kneeling posture and Latch sees his face is alive with anxiety.

"Well, lads, my work is done. Mr. Utterson, help the doctor down. Oh, Eric, are you still here? Will you be so good as to hold the lantern? I'll take the other one."

Startled, the young detective comes closer, obeying John's request.

Poole extends his cane toward Lanyon who puts the handle of his leather bag around the crook and watches its descent onto Henry's shoed feet. Utterson kneels and stretches his arms out to support Lanyon's weight, assisting his friend into the grave .

Lanyon has a hard time positioning his large feet in the limited space at the base of the casket, but Utterson's hands are just able to hold his shoulders steady until Lanyon places one foot on the silk next to Henry's shoe and the other in the earth's soft soil. The doctor is soon able to extract a scissors from the bag and ,with several deft snips, to cut up the sleeve of Jekyll's suit , revealing the arm's flesh. From above they hear him say that the skin is cold and stiff with rigor mortis.

"Perhaps you were right Poole" Lanyon says, "it's good that we made that incision last night. I will try for a direct injection into the heart instead."

Shocked, Eric stares first at his cousin, then nearly drops the lantern as he bends to see the doctor ignore the scissors for this next procedure and forcefully rip the fabric of Jekyll's shirt open to expose the entire torso. A few inches from the corpse's left nipple, a small bandage covers the wound made the night before.

"X marks the spot," says Poole, then adds, "god help us."

With a few swift movements the hulking dark-coated figure below brings the glass syringe into view under the detective's amber light. He pierces Jekyll's breast with its long needle, and pushes down hard on its plunger before withdrawing the instrument from the pectoral muscle. Lanyon looks up at them, his face wet with perspiration, and hurls the bag and its contents up onto the ground. Utterson's arms reach down to pull him to the surface, and soon the four men are standing around the grave looking down at Henry Jekyll, still dead, in silence.

Eric is smoking his pipe. Of course Utterson had figured things entirely right- Poole is undoubtedly just as qualified as Lanyon, or even Jekyll, to practice medicine. And Jekyll, due to the nature of their relationship, would certainly have consulted with him on any number of his patients' ailments over the years. With the office and laboratory right there in the house, Poole would always have easy access to Jekyll's . . .

Poole stoops to pick up his folded coat. The wind has indeed picked up, but Poole is not thinking of himself. Again he employs his cane, this time to lower the coat and drop it as a covering for his friend's bare chest. Now only the face is visible, familiar and yet so very strange to him.

Lanyon inquires about the time. Utterson checks his pocket watch.

"Just after half past eight. We said we'd wait two hours. Do you really think he feels the cold air, Poole?"

"I feel it, Mr. Utterson. I feel it."

The low throbbing cry of the owl nearby in the grove distracts them momentarily, so that when they hear the next sound, a stirring of some sort, they instinctively think its source is also in the bushes.

But it isn't.

Poole's white shirt flies by the others in a flash of blurred movement and dips abruptly out of sight. From the bottom of the grave he cries out instructions.

"On your knees with the lanterns! No need for anyone else down here. Wait! Here. . . here, oh, Henry."

The three above strain their necks, but Poole's head hides Jekyll's face from their view. His soft, gentle words drift upward.

"Oh my dear Henry, my dearest - yes, it is I."

Latch is quick to see a worried, uncomfortable frowning glance pass between Lanyon and Utterson.

"Does he breathe?" asks Lanyon.

Poole's head turns, his face awash with tears of joy.

"Yes, Lanyon, we've done it! Eric, you're a slender fellow. Come down and we'll give Henry a bit of a massage to get his circulation going."

For the first few minutes it's like stroking wooden furniture or the surface of a statue. Jekyll's eyes, however, keep moving back and forth from Eric on one side to Poole on the other. Finally his skin becomes pliant, but his first words are little more than a whisper.

"Why . . .are the three. . . of us . . . in the. . . same bed?"

Above, Utterson wants to know what in Christ's holy name Poole and Latch are laughing about down there. Jekyll is at last lifted from below. Maneuvered gently onto the grass near the lanterns, he possesses the strength of a large rag doll. Lanyon starts, suddenly overcome by a jolt of pain in his shoulder and falls to his knees.

From the nearby bell tower of St. George , nine rich tones pass slowly across the neighborhood. Utterson gazes in the direction of the church.

"We shall pay dearly for all this, gentlemen. I can have no more part in any of it."

He turns, runs and is swallowed up by the shadows.

"Lawyers," grumbles Poole, "they're like scared rabbits, the whole bunch of them. I'm going to carry Henry over to that bench. Eric, you'd better see to Lanyon. He's had a bad heart for years. He should have some pills with him. See if you can take him back to his carriage. Henry and I will wait for you on the bench. Don't forget to come back to us. I'll need help getting him home."

And indeed there is a bench standing in a carefully landscaped curve of grass on the very edge of the nearby grove. Henry groans as Poole half carries, half drags him to it. Eric hands his cousin one of the lanterns, then approaches Lanyon who struggles to his feet.

"A truly miraculous occurrence, my boy!" He is excited but his words are an effort as he leans half his weight against his companion, adding "I shall be famous - think of it!"

Soon he and Eric are seated on the very same bench Eric had sat on earlier with Utterson.

"I fear I shan't make it to the carriage if we don't sit for a spell."

"Poole said something about pills you're supposed to carry. O, goodness! Have we left them back in your bag?"

Lanyon, slurring his words now, says that in all the last minute fussing made at Jekyll's house this afternoon he must have left the pills there.

"No," he adds, "only those infernal potions are in my bag."

"Potions? Plural?"

Mumbling now, Lanyon's chin is actually on the detective's shoulder.

"One vial of my new invention and one containing Jekyll's original. Poole insisted on bringing both. Utterson and I were both anxious about that, I can tell you."

"But surely, Doctor Lanyon, you'd never condone Jekyll transforming himself into Hyde again - not tonight, not after this miracle as you call it? Especially since you personally saw him change into Hyde under your very eyes! Poole claimed Jekyll put on quite an exhibition for you."

With what appear to be the last remnants of his stamina, the doctor feebly grips the lapels of Eric's jacket. His words, though weak, cut like daggers.

"You fool! It wasn't Jekyll who visited me that night to demonstrate the potion - it was Poole!"

Eric quickly stands ramrod straight for the first time since saluting his commanding officer just before leaving India.

Lanyon goes on, still slumped on the bench.

———

172

"Jekyll did of course invent the drug, certainly did most of the work anyway, but when he observed the horrible effects it had on his chimpanzees, he threatened to shut the whole endeavor down. Poole's influence over the man was quite powerful - dominant I would say in the end. One night Jekyll threatened to burn his laboratory journal along with the first batch of his potion. According to Jekyll, Poole grabbed the beaker out of his hand and drank most of it down on the spot."

Overwhelmed by a profound betrayal and a deep shame at allowing himself, as a Scotland Yard detective, to be so taken in by a - well, yes, a criminal, Eric continues,

"Then everything John told me yesterday regarding Jekyll's transformations was a lie! He confessed Jekyll's suicide was due to his not being able to live with the guilt of murdering Sir Carrew. I took a very detailed statement from him. He claimed it was Jekyll who changed repeatedly into this monster."

Eric cannot but marvel at the extent of his cousin's duplicity.

Lanyon, too, spoke with a distinct intensity.

"Henry took his life because he created the potion that allowed Poole to sink into moral depravity. Poole has always been a very clever fellow. You probably never came to know him the way Utterson and I did. So that once Henry was dead - I suppose it was an easy way for him to put the blame on his friend. No, no, your cousin was Edward Hyde all along. It was always him. Poor Henry was afraid to drink the very substance he'd created, and the whole matter positively broke his heart. I can't tell you how many times Henry begged him to cease drinking the potion. Jekyll, thank the good lord, continued to be repulsed by his discovery, but not that other one. As Hyde, Poole thrived - and believed - and no doubt still does, that he can entice Jekyll to follow his lead - join him in his depravity in a new life together for both of them. A life such as that, with both of them having access to that abominable potion - why it would make their past scandalous activity look like a fairy tale!"

Lanyon pleads with Eric to leave him there on the bench and implores him to go back to the grave to retrieve the black bag before something terrible happens.

**********   ************   **********

Chapter SIX

On the bench, in the shadows of the trees behind them, and no more than twenty feet from the recently disturbed grave, sits Poole with his arm around Jekyll's shoulder. He touches some strands of blond curly hair near Jekyll's ear and is visibly upset when his friend pulls away.

"Stop pawing at me like that. If you want to help me, isn't there some whiskey here somewhere? Can't you give me a drink?"

Poole finds the flask in Utterson's coat and hands it to Henry as he reclaims his seat.

"Lovely moon tonight, Henry. And warm. I'm reminded of our holidays in Brighton."

Jekyll groans, takes a long drink, then bends and holds his head in his hands and coughs a few times before sitting up to respond.

"*I'm* reminded that as soon as I feel the strength to move, I'm going straight to the police."

Poole fidgets nervously with the cufflinks at the end of his sleeves.

"Oh yes, you'll have your punishment, won't you? Just like you. Well, I already took care of that yesterday. Went to the Yard and told my cousin Eric you're the evil fiend who invented the potion, changed into Hyde and killed old Carew. Oh, Henry, you should have heard the way I went on, and him taking down every word. Cousin Eric was always such a gullible ass. Why, I made it sound as though everything I did was done by you. I felt like an actor in front of the footlights, just as I've always acted the part of your butler."

"John," begins Jekyll, "I'm exhausted, and my mind is in a jumble. There are many things I can't remember .You should have left me dead tonight, but the truth is I do feel Lanyon's wonder drug is wearing off, and what a blessing it would be if it would. My own open grave's an inviting sight over there."

Henry lays his hand on John's knee and continues.

"You and I can't go on like this . . . it is surely over, whatever was between us. We've both changed too drastically. I no longer know you, and you no longer know me. We need to separate; each must go his own way and accept what comes."

Henry withdraws his hand, noting the growing panic in Poole's eyes.

"Henry, we could have such fun together - now I've learned how to manage the doses. It's the timing that's so important, you know, gauging the right interval between doses. The two of us can easily manage it. And we could travel so much, live wherever we choose. Utterson will let you draw as much money from your funds as we'd need. We could live comfortably and spend our nights howling at that moon up there."

Poole wipes a tear from the corner of his eye.

"Yes, like the beasts we would be, John. You made the same argument not long before I took the morphine. Give me another swig from that flask."

"How am I to live without you?"

"Sounds to me you'd already begun yesterday to do just that."

"You were dead, Henry. I never dreamed that idiot Lanyon's tinkering with your formula would actually work."

"Give me that drink and just go away. I've grown weary of everyone, especially you."

"Very well then," says Poole. "I'll have one with you - is it to be a farewell toast, then, Henry?"

"This seems the perfect place for one, don't you think?"

Poole hands the flask to Henry, bends over the side of the bench and opens Lanyon's bag. He removes a vial filled with a brownish liquid, pulls out the cork stopper and swallows half of it. Jekyll, seeing what he's done, shakes his head in disbelief.

"You haven't!"

************* *********

Chapter SEVEN

Eric is stumbling in almost complete darkness, doing his best to avoid tombstones. He trips once, but when he gets up can't quite fathom in which direction to proceed. Gazing back, he no longer sees the row of gaslights on the sidewalk in front of the hotel. Realizing it was a mistake to leave the cobblestone path, he resorts to stooping and groping with his hands to prevent more collisions. Overhead, clouds shift, causing the moon to shed her light again. Squinting, he thinks he can barely see the clump of trees near Jekyll's grave. But there are voices, and other muffled noises that sound like a struggle. Almost blindly, he heads toward the grove, now making out a lantern's glow through the bushes. He is approaching the grave from the far side - how has he become so disoriented?

The white shirted figure lifts Henry from the bench, slams him to the ground and sits on his mid-section.

"Observe one last time, Henry, the results of your labors!"

Jekyll looks up, helpless, as he sees lumps of muscle and bits of bone and cartilage under Poole's neck and face begin to shift. The eyes bulge, hair thickens, teeth enlarge and twist the mouth into a bestial snarl. With the strength of an animal dragging its prey, Hyde, for that's who it is now, pulls Jekyll closer to the grave. He uses his free hand to pick up the long cane, then turns, lets out a roar and rains down a series of savage blows on Jekyll's head. He stops abruptly and,with a malicious grin, pulls Henry's shirt open.

"Oh, I know where this cane wants to go next - where Lanyon's been poking around! But your heart belongs to me, Henry! Always has, always will!"

His voice, barely human now, seems more like a growl.

"Third time's the charm, Henry - X marks the spot!"

Holding the crook tight with both hands, he pushes the cane's point down hard through the bandage that still covers Jekyll's heart. Hyde's final thrust lowers the point at least six inches down through the tissue and muscle til he feels the cane plant itself in the soil beneath. This final assault produces no response from Jekyll but a blank stare and stillness. Hyde finally realizes his blows to the head had no doubt already killed him.

Eric scrambles frantically from the branches, derringer in his extended hand. The creature, angrily interrupted in the midst of its pleasure, lunges quickly at the intruder, who pulls the trigger. The gun misfires wildly, and Hyde, though momentarily distracted, springs on his cousin with a cry of triumph. He pulls his powerful arm back and delivers a shattering punch to Eric's stomach. Throttled and slammed back and forth, Eric notices, however, the familiar white shirt and makes a mental leap of painful recognition.

"John!" he cries out, nearly doubled over in pain, "my god, is it you?"

Startled, the malformed creature pauses, then suddenly sees the granite monument within easy reach and vigorously pulls the stone head from the angel's shoulder.

"Greetings from your guardian angel, Eric!"

But before he can pulverize his face with the granite weight, Billy charges into view from the grove of trees like a crazed forest elf. Hyde, quick to sense an intruder, jerks around too late to escape the crushing blow from Billy's shovel smashing the side of his head.

Eric is gasping for air that will not come. Billy, instantly recognizing the detective from this morning, rushes to his aid. Out of the corner of his eye, Eric sees that Hyde, on the ground, has begun to stand, and alerts Billy with a warning gesture. Without missing a beat, the gravedigger targets Hyde again, this time mercilessly. With one last blow to his forehead, the shovel unleashes a spray of blood into the night breeze, and the monster falls.

Near the main gate new shadowy movements of men scatter and advance, having heard, from down by the grove, the two men crying for assistance. Utterson is in the forefront, accompanied by several bobbies carrying their bullseye lamps. The piercing shrieks of their whistles reach Eric's ears just before he collapses against Billy's shoulder.

Chapter EIGHT

"Mummy says you're a detective."

Eric was only now coming out of a faint or unconscious state, having been earlier placed on the couch in the lounge by the hotel doorman.

"Is it true - Mummy says you're a detective."

Eric opened his eyes. It was the little boy from the funeral, Jekyll's nephew.

"I'm Donny, though I prefer Don."

"Well, then Don it shall be. I see you still have your green hat on."

He removed it with a nervous energy, exposing a bunch of golden curls.

"I saw you," he said, "at the cemetery this morning."

"Yes," said Eric, "My condolences on your loss."

"Uncle Henry was a good man. He bought me this hat."

A woman in a lovely blue dress flowed into the lounge, a cool breeze accompanying her from the front door.

"In Brighton," added Susan Dodge.

"Mummy, this is a detective."

"Yes, we met this morning."

Eric made an effort to stand, but she startled him by coming nearer and sitting close to him on the couch.

"You mustn't tax yourself, Mr. Latch. I hear one of those brutes gave you quite a pummeling. Our family lawyer tells me that the caretaker tried his best to break it up too, but that the two men killed each other. It's so odd, don't you think, that something so peculiar should happen in there on the very first night of Henry's burial."

The little fellow was going into a fit of excitement with all the talk of fighting and killing, but it did allow Eric the opportunity to evade this last issue Susan had raised.

"O, Mummy, can't we go outside and see the bobbies and -"

"Mr. Latch, I'm afraid my son always needs an adventure."

"Come here, Don. I can tell you something exciting about my time in India."

Mrs. Dodge, animated now herself, involuntarily jerked her hand toward Eric.

"You've been to India, sir?"

"Indeed, served in the army four years. An injury I received there was the reason I needed to see your brother."

"Oh, yes, you did mention something this morning about that."

She bowed her beautiful head in sadness.

"My poor husband died there. . . of malaria, in a place called Agra."

"Ah, yes, I know it. The Taj Mahal is there, I think."

Her son came over closer to Eric and whispered that this is where she always cries a little, but that he shouldn't get upset.

Still keeping her head down but speaking, Eric felt, very deliberately, she went on:
"I can't help worrying that - especially after today- Donny will have no male figure to look up to for guidance."

A few minutes later, Utterson entered, immediately followed by Lanyon. Both, appeared noticeably revived, and Eric was delighted to see the doctor up and about. The two gentlemen urged Mrs. Dodge and the boy to retire to their room for the night and promised to call on her in the morning to drive them to Trent Square to get a look at the house that would soon be legally hers. Assuring her that everything in the cemetery was fine now and that the incident had occurred nowhere near her brother's grave, she and her son started to leave for the lobby.

"Mummy," said the lad, "can't you give the detective our address so he'll come to tell us stories about India?"

Susan blushed only slightly and withdrew a calling card from a little gray purse she'd been carrying. She handed it to him with a smile.

"Mr. Latch, we'll be here at home in the city til June fifteenth, after that we'll be in Bournemouth until mid July visiting some friends. I don't intend to move into Henry's house until the end of the summer. So do try to visit us before we leave for Bournemouth."

Eric replied she could positively count on that.

As soon as she and the boy had gone upstairs, Utterson and Lanyon quickly became somber and drew three chairs near the fireplace. The warmth from its flames created a cozy atmosphere, but it was clear they had something to say to Eric in confidence. It was the doctor who was first to speak.

"I fear, Eric, that Utterson and I have taken some drastic measures just now," and he flashed a worried look at his friend who quickly took over as messenger.

"It's all been done not only to cover our reputations - including your own, by the way - but also to avoid disgracing the family name of Mrs. Dodge - "

" - who does seem -" interrupted Lanyon, "rather taken with you, Mr. Latch."

"What have you done?" asked the detective.

The lawyer took a breath and continued.

"The gravedigger is now, even as we speak, re-burying Henry, and we thought it best to have Poole - though his corpse is stamped with the monstrous features of Hyde - to have IT buried with Jekyll."

Though Eric's astonishment was immediate and palpable, he kept himself in check and reached in his jacket pocket for his pipe. He was surprised to find it still there after the fracas in the graveyard - his tobacco and matches, too.

The two gentlemen looked on as he went through the ritual of lighting up and taking his first puffs.

"Well of course," he finally replied, "someone in my family will eventually report John as missing?"

"We thought," said Utterson, "perhaps YOU could do that. . . in a week or so. People disappear all the time, you see, and an unmarried fellow with his proclivities - if you get my drift, detective - his absence shouldn't create more than a ripple of interest."

Lanyon and Utterson both noted something was still not quite right with their man from the Yard.

"What else is troubling you, Mr. Latch?"

"May I presume, Mr. Utterson, that I might claim you as my lawyer?"

"It would be an honor to represent you in any matter."

"In that case," began Eric, "last night I wrote a report about everything John told me about this whole affair. . ."

Troubled looks darted between Lanyon and Utterson.

"And I was wondering what you might advise me to do with it."

"Burn it," he quickly fired back. "I would advise you to burn it."

Eric nodded his head and posed another question.

"And Billy? Oughtn't we to do something for him?"

"I gave him a large gratuity for his extra work tonight."

"He most certainly saved my life - heroically. Isn't there a bit more we can do for him?"

"Such as?" Utterson inquired.

"A position as clerk of some sort at your offices, sir, or perhaps even at the Yard , since Chief Inspector Soames is a friend of yours?"

"Quite a leap up the ladder for a gravedigger, isn't it, Latch?" Lanyon asked.

"Now, now," cautioned the lawyer, "stranger things have happened."

"Yes, indeed," agreed Lanyon. "We all know that's true enough."

A long pause ensued, as the fire in the hearth crackled near them.

*******************   *****************

Chapter NINE

Bournemouth seemed every bit as charming a coastal resort town as Eric had heard it was. Even more charming, however, was the sight of Susan and Donny waiting for him on the platform when his train arrived that sunny afternoon. In the weeks since the night in the graveyard, he had seen her three times- most recently an afternoon at the British Museum. It was then she suggested he join her for a weekend out here while she and her son were the guests of her friends ,who had not long ago rented a house not far from a stretch of beach. In it there would easily be room to accommodate Susan's new detective friend for a couple of days.

As he stepped down from his car, he noted Donny was wearing an odd looking red and black bandanna around his head as well as a dark smudge just over his lip. But it was the perfect prettiness of Susan who arrested his attention.

A little sprig of lilac was tucked just inside a pink ribbon that circled the brim of her yellow bonnet. Her cheeks seemed dabbed with just the slightest touch of powder or rouge. And her dress was also yellow and of a light material flecked with pale pink blossoms. Eric was absolutely transported by the notion that she had gone to so much trouble to look attractive for him, while here he was walking at her side, carrying his brown leather overnight luggage and, regrettably, attired in his bland gray suit and his black bowler hat.

She was keeping up a lot of chatter about Bobbie, who was a childhood friend and, for a time, of Henry's too. They'd been neighbors, you see, Bobbie's father was a lighthouse keeper in Edinburgh, on a spot of land no more than a rock, known as Skerryvore : " As I told you in London, Eric, his wife's name is Fanny - she's an American who's been married before, and poor Bobbie's changed so much since the last time I saw him. He's always got this dreadful cough - oh, it's not contagious, but it's really the reason they moved out here. His doctors think the sea air might do him a world of good. He's become famous lately, you know."

"How much farther is their house, Susan? This bag weighs a ton and the sun is boiling. . . Famous how?"

"He's a writer. See the book Donny's carrying?"

"Yes, and why has he got that silly handkerchief wrapped round his head on such a hot day? And isn't that a fake moustache smeared above his lip?"

"Oh, Eric," sighed Susan. "He's been waiting for you to notice his get-up, but now you're cross and I'm afraid you've spoiled his fun."

The boy had been marching just ahead of them, but turned now with an announcement:

"Yo -ho - ho and a bottle of rum."

Putting his hands on his hips, he was attempting some sort of a drunken swagger.

"I'm a pirate - Long John Silver! And if you were a good detective you'd have figured it out right away."

He held the book up for view.

"Treasure Island," said Eric approvingly, "First rate title, I'd say. You know, Don, I've got a little pistol my old uncle once told me looked just like a pirate once owned it. And when you're a little older maybe your mother will permit me to give it to you. How does that sound, Mr. Silver?"

"Sounds fine, matey!"

"Oh my," said Susan, "you haven't lost your ability to win him over."

"Though it's his mother I'd much rather. . ." He reached his arm gently round her waist and drew her to him, smiling.

"So your old friend Bobbie wrote that book! Come to think of it, I think I may have seen stacks of them in some London book shop windows the past few weeks."

An attractive dark haired woman was running down the street to meet them, an entirely different type of beauty for him to contemplate. A good many years older than Susan, he thought, with a figure best described as generous, and wearing no bonnet whatsoever. Looking only at her new guest, she held both her arms open for him. He, however, resisted the urge toward informality and instead merely shook her hand.

But she wouldn't let go, smiled playfully at both him and Susan and ushered them around a corner toward a thatch-roofed cottage that lookied very much like it belonged in a fairy tale. Nailed to the trunk of a tree just inside the hedge was a wooden sign with the singular word "Skerryvore" painted on it in red letters. Eric could just make out a garden in the back where a man sat in a wicker chair. He seemed to be sleeping. When their dark haired guide also noticed this, she halted their progress.

"Eric Latch, I am Fanny Stevenson, and I regret to say my husband has the irritating social habit of falling asleep at the most awkward times. I'm certain it's part of the many illnesses he endures. But, trust me, he is very eager to meet you, sir."

"As am I, Mrs. Stevenson, to meet him. Especially now that my pirate friend here, Mr. Silver, has told me about Treasure Island."

Don was beaming now, restrained only by his mother's firm hold from dashing toward the garden.

"Susan and her child are just what Bobbie's needed here this summer, and now with you here too, Mr. Latch, it'll be perfect. When Susan mentioned you're a detective, my husband's face lit up."

"I can't think why."

"Sometimes he needs a jolt of inspiration from a stranger, a scrap of conversation, a bit of family gossip or - well, just about anything that will make his writer's mind click, you see. A detective such as yourself should have at least a couple of stories to tell."

The boy, totally lost in his own imaginings, hooted his refrain which Eric feared they would be hearing frequently in the days to come:

"Fifteen men on a dead man's chest

 Yo - ho - ho and a bottle of rum!"

Eric winked at Fanny and replied that yes, he might know one or two.

And it was Fanny who turned and released Donny to scamper into the garden where the man in the wicker chair sat dozing in the sunlight.

EPILOGUE

In 1885 Robert Louis Stevenson and his American wife Fanny did move into a cottage in Bournemouth, a popular resort town on the south coast of England. He christened their new home Skerryvore in memory of his father's lighthouse in Edinburgh. The author, already famous from the recent success of Treasure Island, is known to have regularly received visitors there. He claimed that the idea for The Strange Case of Dr. Jekyll and Mr. Hyde came to him one night in a feverish dream. Although seriously ill from a nearly life-long respiratory ailment that would only worsen as his remaining years passed, he finished , incredibly, the first draft of the story in three days; according to his wife the manuscript ran to thirty thousand words. She and her ten year old son Lloyd, from a previous marriage, sat down to listen to him read it aloud.

To say that her reaction to this reading is the only reason we have the world famous novella today in its present form is not at all an overstatement. According to her son's account some years later, Fanny had hated it, more or less accusing her husband of writing a superficial thriller, and that he "had missed the allegory completely." Two or three days of considerable tension ensued at Skerryvore.

Then one morning the author, still ill of course, came downstairs and calmly admitted her criticisms had been correct. Fanny seems to have been a forceful, intelligent and perceptive woman; and clearly her husband valued her opinions concerning his craft. Mother and son watched in amazement , however, as he burned the original manuscript in the stove without any discernible fuss or resentment on his part. Returning to his sick bed, no doubt with a supply of pens, ink and paper, he emerged - again reportedly three days later - with the new text of the story. With only some minor edits and revisions, this is the version we have today.

Could Fanny Stevenson's use of the word "allegory" also perhaps illuminate her husband's behavior during those days? As a "teller of tales" did he also want to be seen as a destroyer of them as well? Was he, on some level, caught up in a fanciful stage performance - though for a decidedly limited audience of two - of a play designed to illustrate his power? Whatever the case, it cannot be argued that his artistic powers during that week or two were impressive.

Finally, of course, in Stevenson's tale Poole is Jekyll's devoted butler, little more than an interesting minor character. From the very beginning , however, critics noticed that the story is populated by a group of mature men propelling events along in a world almost totally devoid of women. This, coupled with the vagueness of whatever Hyde's wicked deeds are [aside from the brutal murder of Danvers Carew - though even here critics have suggested homosexual behavior could be at work] readers can easily sense that provocative things may be going on beneath the surface in the lives of these Victorian gentlemen. And isn't that precisely what Dr. Jekyll's shocking research and discovery - as well as Stevenson's great masterpiece itself - is all about?

THE END

jh

Acknowledgment

These novellas would never have seen the light of day without the skills and computer wizardry of Daniel and Margaret Fedor, my lifelong friends. They guided the stories, like the good shepherds they are, to the bright pastures of publication.

Cover created by Margaret and Daniel Fedor

About The Author

Born in Wilkes-Barre, Pennsylvania, in 1947, John Holmes graduated from that city's King's College as an English major in 1969. He received his master's degree from Wilkes University several years later. His career as a teacher spanned thirty-seven years as an English instructor at Bishop Hoban High School. He is currently enjoying his retirement.

Always a lover of literature and films, he has spent most of his life writing various types of fiction that reflect those interests. Primarily writing for his own amusement, he is grateful now for the opportunity to share his latest endeavors with others.

Made in United States
North Haven, CT
19 February 2022

16252992R00114